RAMIREZ AND THE NEARLY DEPARTED

"A fun and lyrical exploration of what it means to find your true talent while keeping your priorities straight.... **A stunning debut by a rising talent.**"

—**DAVID BOWLES**, Pura Belpré Honor–winning author of *They Call Me Güero*

"**Hilarious and heartfelt.**... A musical, food-filled party for the artist in everyone!"

—**CARLOS HERNANDEZ**, Pura Belpré Award–winning author of *Sal and Gabi Break the Universe*

"**A funny and heartwarming story about family, friendship,** and discovering your talents that resonates like a beautiful song."

—**CHRISTINA DIAZ GONZALEZ**, Edgar Award–winning author of *Concealed*

"**A humorous and haunting riff** on a classic storyline."

—*KIRKUS REVIEWS*

"Benny's story is **a charming, not-scary ghost story** with moments of joy, sadness, and wishing-you-were-there in Miami eating a delicious Cubano sandwich."

—*SCHOOL LIBRARY JOURNAL*

ALSO BY JOSÉ PABLO IRIARTE

AJ Torres and the Treasure of Captain Grayshark

BENNY RAMÍREZ AND THE NEARLY DEPARTED

JOSÉ PABLO IRIARTE

A YEARLING BOOK

A Yearling Book
An imprint of Random House Children's Books
A division of Penguin Random House LLC
1745 Broadway, New York, NY 10019
penguinrandomhouse.com
rhcbooks.com

Text copyright © 2024 by Working Partners Ltd
Cover art and interior illustrations copyright © 2024 by Mirelle Ortega

All rights reserved. Published in the United States by Yearling, an imprint of Random House Children's Books, a division of Penguin Random House LLC, New York. Originally published in hardcover in the United States by Alfred A. Knopf, an imprint of Random House Children's Books, a division of Penguin Random House LLC, New York, in 2024.

Yearling and the jumping horse design are registered trademarks
of Penguin Random House LLC.

The Library of Congress has cataloged the hardcover edition of this work as follows:
Names: Iriarte, José Pablo, author.
Title: Benny Ramírez and the nearly departed / José Pablo Iriarte.
Description: New York : Alfred A. Knopf, 2024. | Audience: Ages 8–12. |
Summary: Twelve-year-old Cuban American Benny must help the ghost of his rich, famous, and morally bankrupt musician grandfather cross over to the other side before the New Year's Eve deadline.
Identifiers: LCCN 2023038504 (print) | LCCN 2023038505 (ebook) |
ISBN 978-0-593-70370-0 (hardcover) | ISBN 978-0-593-70371-7 (library binding) |
ISBN 978-0-593-70372-4 (ebook)
Subjects: CYAC: Grandfathers—Fiction. | Music—Fiction. | Future life—Fiction. |
Family life—Fiction. | Cuban Americans—Fiction. | Humorous stories. |
LCGFT: Humorous fiction. | Novels.
Classification: LCC PZ7.1.I75 Be 2024 (print) | LCC PZ7.1.I75 (ebook) |
DDC [Fic]—dc23

ISBN 978-0-593-70373-1 (pbk.)

Printed in the United States of America
10 9 8 7 6 5 4 3 2
First Yearling Edition 2025

The authorized representative in the EU for product safety and compliance is Penguin Random House Ireland, Morrison Chambers, 32 Nassau Street, Dublin D02 YH68, Ireland, https://eu-contact.penguin.ie.

Random House Children's Books supports the First Amendment
and celebrates the right to read.

Penguin Random House values and supports copyright. Copyright fuels creativity, encourages diverse voices, promotes free speech, and creates a vibrant culture. Thank you for buying an authorized edition of this book and for complying with copyright laws by not reproducing, scanning, or distributing any part of it in any form without permission. You are supporting writers and allowing Penguin Random House to continue to publish books for every reader. Please note that no part of this book may be used or reproduced in any manner for the purpose of training artificial intelligence technologies or systems.

TO LISA, OF COURSE

BENNY RAMÍREZ AND THE NEARLY DEPARTED

PROLOGUE

Ignacio Ramírez would never describe himself as a great artist. He was far too humble for that. He was the humblest artist he knew, and he knew many, being a famous musician himself. Anybody who came into Ignacio's living room, where he now stood with his trumpet, working on his soon-to-be amazing comeback song, would know how great he was. They would know from the gold records on the walls, from the Latin Grammy on the mantel for his big hit, "Miami Maravilloso," and from the photographs of his glory days with anybody who was anybody en el negocio. Ignacio Ramírez didn't need to tell anyone what a great artist he was, because his walls would do it for him.

And once he figured out how to end this new song, his music would remind the world that he was numero uno.

Ignacio lifted his trumpet to his lips and played the beginning notes of his comeback composition. Eight measures in, he unleashed his secret weapon: the double high C that was his trademark, a note few trumpet players could hit at all, let alone with the screaming force that he packed. The force that would carry him back to the top.

He had been holding the note for several seconds, imagining the critics losing their minds at his latest masterpiece, when a tightening sensation in his chest took his breath away. Pain shot down his left arm, and Ignacio staggered to one knee.

By the living room window, his dog, Iggy 2, lifted his head and huffed.

Ignacio winced but waved off the dog's concern. "No te preocupes, Iggy. I'm fine. It's just—it's just—"

Another throb shot through him.

"—gas," he concluded weakly. "I shouldn't have had all those frijoles negros with lunch today!"

A spotlight hit him just then—wait, a spotlight? Here in his living room? He loved the idea, but he was sure he had never installed such a thing. He looked up and saw that it was no spotlight, but a tunnel, made of brilliant white light.

"Ay," he said softly. "It's not frijoles, is it?"

Without getting up, without being conscious of walking or doing anything at all, Ignacio entered the tunnel. It felt like it stretched on forever, and also passed by in an instant, like life, until he reached the end, where he found . . . a door?

It was the most ordinary of wooden doors, painted white, with shoe scuffs at the base and a peephole at eye level. From the other side came rhythmic sounds . . . music, Ignacio realized. Horns and percussion mixed with cheers and laughter. Ignacio took in a deep breath, and the aroma of roast pork tickled his taste buds.

He was dead? And death was . . . a party?

This didn't sound so bad. Of course, there had been so much he still wanted to do, but if this was his fate, well, Ignacio had never turned down a party in his life. In fact, he had been known all his days as the life of the party, though he would never tell anybody that, because he was much too modest.

He reached out for the door, preparing to announce his presence and bask in the applause.

But before he could close his hand around the dented brass knob, the door swung open. The light on the other side was blinding, so much so that it took Ignacio a moment to see the figure in the doorway, blocking him from entering.

"Ignacio Ramírez!" said a familiar voice. "I knew someday I'd see you trying to crash this party!"

Back out in the tunnel, it became easier to see, and Ignacio realized he knew this man. "Francisco! My old piano player! What a wonderful surprise!" A quick movement at the man's feet caught Ignacio's attention, and he looked down to see a beagle. "And . . . is that Iggy 1? My old dog!"

The man shook his head, frowning. "No, I'm Carlos. I played drums. Francisco played timbales."

Ignacio waved the correction away. "Of course, of course! It's been so many years! But we're all here now! This will be wonderful. Just like the parties back in the day!"

Iggy 1 bared his teeth and growled as Ignacio tried to edge his way in.

The other man put out a hand. "Not so fast! *You* definitely do not deserve to come to this party."

"What?" Ignacio tugged on his jacket lapels. "How could you say that, uh . . . Antonio? I'm a star! You can't have a party without a star! My music is beloved. Come on . . . compadre, let's add some pizzazz to this party!"

"You, a star? Your *one* hit plays in all the best elevators."

Ignacio gasped. Had this insolent fool really just insulted the most famous, brilliant musician of his time? "What? How dare—"

"And my name is *Carlos*. Antonio was a dancer. And I say you don't belong."

Iggy 1 huffed in agreement as the door inched shut.

Ignacio's heartbeat drummed in his ears. Or was that the bongos from inside the party? Did he even *have* a heartbeat anymore?

Heartbeat or not, he knew he was facing the end. If he

let that door close, he didn't know what waited for him, but he was sure it was nothing good.

"Wait!" he cried out, sticking his shoe between the closing door and the frame. "Please! I'm begging you! I was not a bad man!"

His former bandmate raised an eyebrow, seeming to consider this. "You think the bar is pretty low, don't you? Were you a *good* man, Ignacio? Did you ever think about the people you left behind? The promises you didn't keep? The help you didn't give?"

Ignacio paused. Honestly, no, he hadn't thought about those things. He'd been so busy being great, he hadn't questioned if he was good. But surely he'd done good things . . . hadn't he? A lump formed in his throat as he rummaged through his brain.

"I raised money for charity!" he cried.

"Benefit concerts where you got paid to perform don't count."

"I did community service!"

"That was literally your sentence for driving on the turnpike at a hundred miles an hour."

"I was a family man!"

"Your wife divorced you, and your own son is not on speaking terms with you."

That brought Ignacio up short. Gloria and Félix had been his world at first. But that was a long time ago, and it had been years since he'd seen his grandchildren. He probably wouldn't recognize them now. Was Pedro right?

"Give me a chance!" Ignacio sobbed. "Let me show you I belong!"

Iggy 1 huffed dismissively, but the man whose name was definitely not Pedro chewed his lower lip, considering. "I don't believe you can," he said at last, "which is why it costs me nothing to give you some time to prove yourself. You have unfinished business in the land of the living, Ignacio. Figure out what it is and resolve it by . . . let's say New Year's. Prove that you're not completely rotten and we'll let you in. If not, you'll be trapped forever in the place where you died. Alone and invisible, for all of eternity."

"Thank you so much, Julio!" Ignacio gushed, gripping the other man's arm. He'd known he would not end up shut out in the cold. Not *him*. Not the great Ignacio Ramí—"Wait a minute! New Year's? That's only four months away! That's not fair!"

His onetime bandmate raised a corner of his lip. "Life is not always fair, Ignacio. And, I suppose, neither is death."

With that he shut the door, and Ignacio tumbled backward down the tunnel of light.

CHAPTER ONE

If there was a worse way to wake up than crammed into the backseat of an SUV with your brother and sister at the end of a fourth straight day on the road, then I never wanted to experience it. One minute I was dreaming about accepting an award for . . . well, *something*. The next I was getting shoved rudely by my younger brother, Manny.

"Stay on your side, bro," he said. "You drool when you sleep."

"I do *not*," I replied, wiping my chin off with my T-shirt.

He ignored me and went back to studying his *Little Shop of Horrors* script. Other people read books. Manny memorized scripts. For fun.

"I'll be so glad when I'm not stuck with you two cavemen," my sister, Cristina, said without glancing up from her phone. She had such an attitude ever since she turned thirteen, even though she was *still* only a year older than me.

"Manny, Benny, Cristina, basta," my mother said. "We're almost there."

I peered out the window. When did we get off the interstate? At some point while I slept, the billboards, mile markers, and rest stops had been replaced by palm trees, traffic lights, and pastel-colored buildings.

I looked at the GPS up front. ETA: sixteen minutes! We really *were* almost at our new home.

Everything was going to be different. New house. New town. New school.

The GPS lady told us to turn left, and within a couple of blocks, the traffic and businesses gave way to massive trees that covered the road in a canopy so thick it felt like night underneath, though it was only late afternoon.

This . . . looked nothing like the pictures of Miami I'd seen online. Where were the pink-and-aqua buildings? Where were the high-rise towers? Where was the beach? Instead, it seemed like we were driving into an urban jungle. The sidewalks wound around the gnarly tree trunks like they'd lost a turf war, and even the street had bumps where the roots had managed to lift the asphalt. Joggers and bicyclists dodged each other on the roller-coaster pavements, and I peered past them at massive houses, wondering if the people who lived inside were all famous like Abuelo had been.

We'd never visited Abuelo at his home. The few times I'd

seen him involved awkward meals when his tours or television appearances brought him out to California. Somehow, I'd imagined he spent all his days on a sandy beach and all his nights in neon-lit clubs dancing to rumba, merengue, and cha-cha-cha. Now I stared hungrily at the passing walkways, trying to mentally put him into the picture I was seeing, as though then I might know him better than I did when he was alive.

A few more turns brought us to a fancy black gate with gold-colored musical notes set between iron bars. Papi pulled up to a keypad mounted on a stand and typed in the code Guillermo had sent last week. The gates swung open. Was this the entrance to his subdivision?

The street turned from asphalt to reddish brown bricks laid in a crisscross pattern. My eyes widened as I looked ahead. The driveway dead-ended at a single enormous building with beige walls and a tiled roof the color of saffron. This wasn't Abuelo's *neighborhood*. This was his *house*.

Papi pulled in next to the single car in the driveway, an old green compact with rust spots on the hood and roof. Once the SUV rolled to a stop, Cristina pushed the door open and we hopped out. Somehow, it was more real without a window separating me from this . . . *mansion*.

I bounced on my toes. "We're gonna live *here*?"

Papi had told us the house had five bedrooms, so I expected it to be a *little* bigger than our three-bedroom home in Los Angeles. You could fit at least three of our old house in here, though. Plus, it had an ocean view straight out of a swanky travel ad. My first glimpse of the Atlantic Ocean, and it was from the driveway of my new home!

I turned back toward Manny, who had staggered out behind me. "Check it out!"

He shrugged.

Cristina came around the other side. "It's a bit extra, no?"

I stared at her. "What?"

Mami slammed her door and popped the trunk. "Vamos," she said. "Ayuden."

I followed Cristina and Manny to the back, where we each grabbed a piece of luggage. While Manny and I grunted with effort, Cristina swung her suitcase out of the trunk with ease. Her suitcase outweighed both of ours, but she was taller than us, and strong from all her dancing.

The sun touched the tops of the trees, and the light pouring out through the large windows of the house made it dazzle like a jewel. It resembled a Spanish castle, with round turrets flanking a tall door.

Papi stretched beside the SUV's front grille, and then trudged up the driveway. "I swear, Ignacio's house must be a half hour from the nearest grocery store."

Since I could remember, Papi called his father by his first name. I tried to imagine calling my father Félix but could not even form the word in my mouth. It was too weird.

The door opened as we approached, and an older man I

had not seen since Manny's First Communion stepped out. My grandfather's buddy, Guillermo.

"Bienvenidos," he called.

"Hola, Guillermo," my father replied.

My throat dried up as my family and I climbed the steps to the house. I'd been so preoccupied with the move, I'd hardly thought about the fact that my abuelo, my father's father, had died just last month. In my defense, there hadn't even been a funeral. According to Abuelo's lawyer, he had left instructions for what should be done in the event of his death. Abuelo hadn't seen the point in making funeral arrangements—why plan a party he couldn't attend? Instead, he'd skip the wake and the funeral and take his final bow at the Caballero Rivero Woodlawn North Cemetery, where he would be buried alongside the likes of Fernando Bujones—one of the greatest Cuban American ballet dancers that ever touched the stage. So that's what happened after Abuelo died.

Before that, I'd met him only about three times in my life. I'm pretty sure even though my middle name is Ignacio, after him, he would not have been able to pick me out of a group photo. Papi hardly ever talked to him after Abuelo and Abuela divorced.

But for Guillermo, who'd known Abuelo since before I was born, this had to hurt more.

"Lo siento," I said as he held the door open for me.

"Huh?" he asked. "Sorry for what?"

"Your loss. I know you were close to my grandfather."

"Um," he said. "Sure."

Poor guy. He was so sad, he couldn't talk about it.

Barely two steps into the foyer, I practically crashed into Manny, who stood gawking like we were in the Grand Canyon. Which, fair, the room *was* immense.

"Hello!" I called out, listening to my own voice bouncing back off the ceiling twenty feet above me.

"Oh wow!" said Manny. Then, in what I guess he thought was a deep voice, he added, "'To be . . . or not to be—*that* is the question!'"

"Niños, ¡ya!" Mami interjected. "¡Cállen—"

Her voice fell off as the echo of her own words practically deafened us. "Oh my," she conceded. "That *is* something!"

Cristina did a silent soft-shoe in her sneakers on the marble floor. "I can't wait to dig my old tap shoes out of storage! They would sound amazing here!" She finished with a flourish, grabbing the rail of the humongous staircase and dipping herself.

I followed the staircase up with my eyes. Hardwood steps with a purple carpet running down the center curved around marble columns to an open loft looking down on us. In the middle of the wall above the stairs hung a gigantic painting. I recognized Abuelo's face, but this was a different Abuelo than the one I'd barely known. I was used to seeing the posed studio pictures of him that ended up on magazine covers, but this seemed like a candid moment. He was younger, around Papi's age, and stood on a stage wearing an iridescent purple tuxedo decorated with a silver floral pattern. He held a trumpet against his lips, his cheeks puffed up and his face flushed. Behind him, contrasting sharply against a bright red curtain, were three other men in tuxedos—plain black ones with white shirts, not purple like Abuelo's. One man blew a saxophone, one plucked a guitar, and the third hammered on some kind of xylophone thing. In front of each musician was a lit music stand stamped with the letters *IR*. To Abuelo's left was the curved end of a piano, hinting at even more musicians just out of view. All the men's faces were blurry and indistinct. Only Abuelo was in sharp focus, leaning to his left and pointing the horn up like he was totally lost in the music.

Manny cocked his head. "Abuelo had a painting of *himself*?"

"Why shouldn't he?" I demanded. "He was famous!"

Cristina snorted. "I starred in *Sleeping Beauty* last year, but you don't see me putting pictures of myself everywhere."

"What are you talking about? You are *constantly* taking selfies!"

"That's different. I'm a *dancer*," she said, as if explaining that rain is wet. "Anybody who's *anybody* in the arts needs to be on social media. I don't hang my pictures on my own wall for *me* to look at."

Guillermo cleared his throat. "If you follow me, I will give you the tour. You might want to put your things down first."

He didn't have to ask twice. We all left our luggage in a pile by the door and followed him to the other side of the entry hall. I peered past Guillermo, into a living room with twelve-foot-tall windows. The boxes we'd shipped ahead were stacked in the center, but there was more. *So. Much. More.* It seemed as though every gift a fan, sponsor, or fellow musician ever sent my grandfather had ended up here. Right by the entrance, there was a cardboard display of Abuelo in a guayabera shirt with red-and-orange flames running up the front where the pleats usually went. He held a can, and to the right of him a block of text proclaimed, "I can play for hours, thanks to High Peak Water! What can High Peak do for YOU?"

The display had cardboard shelves where cans of High Peak were supposed to go, all empty except for one, which contained a silver pendant with the words MIAMI MARAVILLOSO in cursive script. If there was anything I knew about my abuelo, it was that "Miami Maravilloso" was the hit that put him on the map. Though these days I mostly heard it as background music in commercials and on elevators.

I stepped into the living room, thinking nothing could beat that, until I saw the mural that had been blocked by the entry. The entire right wall was . . . sheet music. Staffs ran the length of the wall, curving as though they were on a giant piece of paper blowing in the wind, carefully making their way around framed records and posters, including, of all things, one for a Mazda dealership.

On, between, and above the lines, black plastic musical notes literally stuck out of the wall. Along the top, just below the ceiling, was the title "MIAMI MARAVILLOSO, por Ignacio Ramírez." And to the right of the music, the last light of the setting sun came in through a stained-glass cutout in the shape of the Miami skyline.

I was nearly knocked over by Manny crashing into me and then grabbing onto my arm to steady himself.

"Sorry," he said. "I tripped over the alligator."

I blinked and turned toward him. "The . . . alligator?"

Manny pointed. Apparently, I had been too distracted by the sheet . . . uh, *wall* music to notice a life-size ceramic alligator in an unlikely upright stance guarding Abuelo's sofa.

"This is where Iggy spends most of his time," Guillermo said.

Iggy? Had Guillermo called Abuelo that?

And wait—what did he mean by *spends* most of his time?

Before I could ask, Guillermo led us back out of the living room, gesturing toward the primary suite, a study, the family room, and a covered patio with wicker furniture. Then we climbed another set of stairs, and he showed us the doors to four more bedrooms, a game room, and a media room.

While Mami and Papi lagged behind us, debating whether or not to change the lavender carpet installed upstairs, Guillermo crossed the second floor, returning to the grand staircase. On his way down, it almost looked like he glanced up at Abuelo's portrait and rolled his eyes. But I must have imagined it.

I wondered if I could ask Guillermo about Abuelo. He knew him better than any of us, with the possible exception of Papi, who never wanted to talk about his music-star father. Even when Abuela visited us, she would frown and change the subject if anybody mentioned her ex-husband.

But I guess that was something Guillermo had in common with them, because he didn't want to talk about him either. As soon as we followed him back downstairs, and my parents caught up to us, he pulled a set of keys from his pocket and handed them to Papi.

"It's all yours now," he said.

"Won't you stay for dinner?" Mami asked.

He shook his head. "I can't. I'm expected back at my new job."

"New job?"

"Yes, well, Señor Ramírez no longer needs butler services, so . . ." He gave us a one-armed shrug.

I glanced at Cristina. Her eyes were wide, her face mirroring my own thoughts. *Butler?* I mouthed. In interviews, Abuelo had made it sound like Guillermo was his best friend. He hadn't mentioned that he paid him to be.

"Oh," Mami said, blinking. "Oh. Yes. Of course."

"I've only been coming here every day to take care of Iggy," Guillermo went on, "but now he's got you."

"Iggy?" Mami repeated.

I chewed my lip. What did he mean by *take care* of Iggy? Was he *not* talking about Abuelo?

Guillermo gestured toward the living room. "Iggy 2, to be precise. Your father-in-law's dog."

As one, we all turned to the massive room we had stumbled around in just minutes ago. There, among stacks of boxes and leaning memorabilia, a sad-looking beagle stared back at us.

How had I missed a living, breathing *dog*?

Manny scratched his head. "Abuelo named his *dog* after himself?"

Cristina ran to the dog's side. "Hi, Iggy!" she said, her voice pitched higher than Snow White's.

"Cristina, espera," Papi said. "You don't know if that dog's friendly."

But it was too late; Cristina was already petting his scruffy fur. Iggy seemed more indifferent than anything else. He wagged his tail once, half-heartedly, but didn't react much beyond that.

"Ay madre, un perro," Mami said.

"What's wrong with him?" Manny asked. "He seems sad."

"He's been reluctant to eat since his master passed away," Guillermo replied.

At least *somebody* seemed to be missing Abuelo.

Guillermo clasped his hands together. "Anyway," he said, a hint of something genuine in his voice, "welcome to Miami. I'm sure you'll love it here."

He hurried out the door with a spring in his step, the same way I'd walk out of school on the last day before summer vacation.

After a moment, I followed my parents back into the living room.

Manny joined Cristina beside Iggy. "We should train him to be an animal actor. Then I could audition for gigs that want a boy *and* a dog."

Cristina snorted. "The only thing I can see you training this dog to do is lie still on command."

Manny got down on all fours and started whining and bumping heads with Iggy, as though he were a dog trying to make friends. He always did that sort of thing. He was an actor, and to him that meant being confused about where the role ended and real life began. A couple of years ago, in third grade, he was cast as the sun in the school play, and he kept going around staring at things intently and willing them to burn.

"What are we going to do with all this *stuff*?" Mami wondered.

I carefully stepped past all the boxes and a cardboard cutout of Abuelo holding a trumpet and walked to the sofa. Cristina flipped open a binder she spotted on the coffee table, revealing it to be a scrapbook of newspaper clippings and fan letters.

Manny made a face. "Abuelo kept a scrapbook about *himself*?"

"Looks like he was his biggest fan," Cristina replied.

I just shrugged. If I had fan mail or newspaper articles written about me, I would definitely take them out and read them once in a while.

Cristina shut the book. "Papi, this place is a disaster."

"Maybe it's not too late to go back," Manny suggested.

"Yeah," Cristina agreed, "but let's bring Iggy with us."

I practically jumped to my feet. "Go *back*? What, to Los Angeles? Why?"

Why would they want to leave this amazing house, and this chance to learn more about Abuelo? I hadn't been unhappy in L.A., and I still felt nervous about the move, but now that we were here, I was excited about all the new things we would be able to explore in Miami.

Cristina crossed her arms. "I had a part lined up in *Swan Lake*."

"And *I* was gonna be in *Seussical*," Manny added.

Papi held out a hand. "Come on, now, we've talked about this. You'll be in demand right here in Miami. Your whole school is a magnet for the best performers. And with all you both have accomplished in L.A., you're going to be *amazing*."

"But what about our friends?" Cristina whined. "Ava

and Jean are probably planning Rosie's birthday party right now . . . without me!"

I couldn't argue with that. I had friends at my old school too that I was really going to miss. But the sympathetic look on Papi's face said that even though missing our friends was sad, it would not be enough to have us pack up our stuff and drive across the country again.

"You will make new friends here, I promise," he said.

In other words, moving back to L.A. was out. Part of me was relieved we'd be staying put if only because there's no way I could do another road trip squished between my siblings for four days. But the other part of me felt nervous because Papi was right. Manny and Cristina would be fine. The only one who *wouldn't* be in demand was me. A magnet school for performers made sense for them, but I was no artist. South Miami Performing Arts School required most students to audition for a chance to attend. Kids of faculty and staff were given an exception—they could attend the school without trying out and take mostly regular academic classes, but even then, they had to take some arts classes too.

Since they were actually performers, Manny and Cristina had sent in recordings of their audition pieces. I sent in nothing; it was only a matter of time before everybody figured out that the "kids of faculty" policy had gotten me in and that I had no talent of my own.

Cristina flopped down onto an armchair. "I bet the dance productions are so basic."

"Probably not," Papi said. "Miami is a film and television hot spot and has a thriving music scene. I bet all the other arts are flourishing too."

"*Sure* they are," she muttered.

"Listen," he said, "I know this is an enormous change for you. For me as well. Change can be good, though. And with Mom and me working at the school, we'll all get to spend more time together. Won't that be cool?"

I swallowed. I loved Papi and Mami, but they didn't have a firm grasp of what kids thought was cool. Having our parents teach at our school was only a half step above all of us showing up in matching outfits.

Manny shook his head. "Just 'cause Abuelo left you this place didn't mean we needed to actually move here. Why did we have to leave Los Angeles?"

I exchanged a glance with Cristina. Manny hadn't figured it out yet, but the two of us were pretty sure Papi had lost his job. Television producers didn't just leave Hollywood to become teachers—even after inheriting a mansion.

"Actually, I think it'll be terrific having Papi around," I hurried to say.

"That's the spirit," Mami said. "Now, why don't the three of you go pick out your rooms?"

A minute later, after racing Cristina up the stairs and

watching her beat me to the room on the left, I pushed open the next door, hoping not to get blinded by the same lavender walls as Cristina's.

I didn't have to worry. This room had *black* walls, which beat lavender, anyway. Unfortunately, it was even more crowded with stuff than the living room. I guess when you live alone in a giant house, every other space might as well be a closet.

I picked my way past trophies, plaques, and shadow boxes containing signed programs and tickets. . . . Finally, I uncovered a bed. At least I would have someplace to sleep.

From behind me, Manny tugged on my arm. "Wow!" he said. "Once we get all the junk out of here, we're gonna have so much space!"

I stared at him. "What are you talking about?"

"This room. Good choice, bro!"

I bit my lip. "Manny," I said. "The house has five bedrooms."

He blinked. "Yeah, so?"

"So you should go pick one of the other two. You know, to be your *own* room."

His mouth dropped open and his eyes dulled as he backed up a step. "Oh," he said. "Okay."

He walked slowly out the door, to the bedroom in the back, directly over the primary suite. I felt bad, but . . . I always wanted my own room, and I wasn't going to live in a gigantic house and not have one.

Papi stuck his head in the door. "I see you've— Oh, hey. I don't know if you in this room is gonna work, Benny. Everything here seems . . . fragile."

I picked up a stuffed bear wearing a starburst tuxedo jacket and matching bow tie. When I spotted the plastic trumpet in the bear's paw, I realized it was supposed to be Abuelo. "You mean like this?"

"Don't touch!" he cried, as if the bear were made of crystal.

"Come on," I said, poking a mannequin wearing a black IGNACIO RAMÍREZ GIRA MUNDIAL T-shirt. "I won't break anything."

As I held up the mannequin's left hand, the arm fell off, but I caught it before it hit the floor.

Dad grumbled as he took the arm from me and placed it gently on the carpet. "That's what you said right before you broke my Producers Guild award."

Low blow! "It was slippery! Anyway, I was eight then. I'm older now."

Papi sighed. "Will you promise to be careful?"

I held up three fingers. "Scout's honor."

His eyes narrowed, but after several seconds, he nodded. "All right," he said. "Tomorrow morning we'll see about moving these things to the spare bedroom. Go get your suitcase."

I ran downstairs before he could change his mind. While Mami ordered pizzas, Cristina, Manny, and I unpacked.

Well, I cleared out a corner for my things. With that done, I eyed the room. It was so full of Abuelo's treasures from his life as a musician, it was like being in my own personal museum of salsa music. And it was time for a tour.

I promised to *be careful*. I never promised not to *touch* anything.

I moved a heavy bronze sculpture of Abuelo's head out of sight behind a shelf.

Below that were six-packs of Jupiña pineapple soda. I was tempted to taste one, until I pulled a dust-covered can out and saw an illustration on the side of my abuelo blowing his trumpet. This wasn't overflow storage for extra soft drinks—these were *memorabilia*. Abuelo was everywhere!

I couldn't imagine being so great at something, fans would want my image on everything from T-shirts to soda cans. *Must be nice*, I thought.

Nobody else in my family was famous, but they all had gifts. Cristina was a star dancer, the lead in every show. Manny was going to be a movie star someday. He'd already worked in commercials and as an extra sometimes. He could memorize lines instantly and cry on command—something he insisted only the best actors could do. Mami had a talent for languages and used to be an interpreter. She was going to be the Spanish teacher at our new school. She also sang beautifully in the church choir and regularly killed it at karaoke. Papi could play the guitar, and he produced some of the best shows on TV—or at least, he *did* before we left L.A.

The school was lucky to have him as the head of the drama department.

Then there was me. I had two left feet along with hands that were all thumbs, I had never been on stage, and the closest I got to singing was when I stubbed my toe. All I could do was hope that nobody noticed how *un*talented I was. I wished I had even a single thing I was amazing at, so I could fit in.

I wandered through the room, moving aside trophies, gold-painted guitar picks, and a fake highway sign indicating 228 miles to Havana. As I picked up a flyer for one of Abuelo's concerts, packed with quotes about how incredible he was, I tried to figure out what I could do to spare myself some humiliation at school.

I could tell everybody I was allergic to anything artsy and would break out into hives . . . nah, not with my parents around. They'd rat me out for sure. What if I told the other kids I was a scientific genius and that's why I never got into the arts? I did like science. But last year when I did my science fair project, only Cristina's last-minute help kept my erupting volcano from becoming a giant gluey mess.

I growled in frustration and slumped down on the bed. No matter what story I told, it wouldn't help me make friends with kids who were all super talented. They tended to hang out with other kids who were future stars too—like Manny and Cristina. I would just end up being known as their weird talentless brother. It would be great if I could show up and have the other kids like me just for being Benny. But I had a sinking feeling that would only happen if I could also tap-dance down a flight of stairs or play a piano concerto with one hand. I looked at my fingers and tried to picture them dancing gracefully across a row of piano keys, but even in my imagination I was all thumbs.

I glanced around, searching for anything that might spark an idea. That's when I noticed a glass figure on the nightstand. It was in the shape of a musical note and stood on a wooden base.

Turning it around, I found a brass plate with engraving on it: "Hay magia en la música. ¡Qué MARAVILLA! ¡AZUCAR!" Below the words was a reproduction of an autograph, consisting of two large *C*'s with some scribble in between.

I ran a finger over the signature. A tingle ran through me as I touched its surface. The weirdness of this day was finally catching up with me, I thought.

"That was a gift from Celia Cruz," a deep voice said.

I jumped up, tripped over a box of Miami Maravilloso coloring books, then landed on the bed. It sounded like Papi, and for a moment I thought he had come back and busted me handling the mementos. But when I looked up, I saw a skinny man with bushy white hair and deep wrinkles, standing in the shadows by the balcony. He wore . . . a neon-green suit? With rhinestones?

I scrambled to my feet and backed up against the wall

in full-on freak-out mode. A total stranger had broken into my room! If his outfit didn't kill me, his bony hands would. "How did you get in here? If you come anywhere near me, I'll scream!"

The man stepped out into the light, not seeming to pay attention to the tripping hazards that surrounded him. "You can hear me?"

My heart raced as I peered into the same face from the painting above the stairs. *"Abuelo?"*

The musical note slipped from my hands. Everything turned to slow motion as it bounced off the corner of the mattress and sailed through the air.

The man shot a hand up with surprising agility, and for a moment it seemed he would pluck it right out of its arc.

Then the statue passed through his hands as though he weren't there and slammed onto the floor, shattering into a thousand pieces.

CHAPTER TWO

A tingle ran from the small of my back all the way up to my scalp. I picked up the mannequin arm I'd broken earlier and held it in front of me. Brandishing it like a spear, I backed away, legs feeling weak.

"Don't be afraid," the man said. "I am your grandfather. Your abuelo."

I tried to calm my racing thoughts long enough to take in what he'd just said. But it didn't make any sense. It seemed a lot more likely that he was the most unfashionable serial killer ever. Then why did he happen to look exactly like Ignacio Ramírez?

"You can't be," I croaked. "My abuelo's dead." Swallowing,

I added, "There's a cemetery plot with his name on it and everything."

He smiled ruefully. "Unfortunately, yes, my boy. It happened in this very house, in fact."

I took several breaths, none of which seemed to give me any air. Was he straight up saying that he was a . . . a . . . a ghost?

And wait—that he died in my new home?

Great. That was something I did *not* need to know. "Oh."

He nodded. "I was alone, working on my great comeback piece, when—" He snapped a finger and whistled. "Heart attack." He sighed. "Don't have a heart attack, nieto. They're not much fun."

I slid along the wall, which was comfortingly solid. "Got it," I squeaked. Then I added, "No heart attacks," in a voice that was *almost* back in my regular pitch.

I made a mental list: (1) Don't break anything (else); (2) Figure out how to survive school tomorrow; (3) Find out everything there is to know about ghosts; (4) Don't have a heart attack.

Succeeding at that last one seemed a bit iffy, since my own heart was pounding like a jackhammer.

Actually, no. That was the door. Somebody was banging on it.

I hurried over and cracked it open.

Manny stood outside. "Are you okay? I heard a crash."

I turned back to the other side of the door—yep, this ghost or hallucination or zombie was still there, watching me. I couldn't let Manny or anybody else in here until I figured out what was going on and what to do about it.

"Oh. Ha ha," I said, forcing a casual laugh. "I dropped something." I held up the mannequin arm. "That's it. We're all fine here. I mean, *I'm* all fine here, thanks...."

"Can I come in?"

"No!" I took a breath. "I mean, not right now. I'm really busy. Unpacking."

"I can help!" He took a step toward me.

I put up a hand to block him. "Thanks, but I've got this."

Manny blinked. "Oh. Okay. See you later, then."

He turned and wandered back toward his own room.

I felt something thick in my throat as I watched Manny walk away. The last thing I wanted was to make him feel lonely. But what was I supposed to tell him? That he couldn't come in because there was a ghost in my room and three's a crowd?

I closed the door and turned away from it, my legs feeling like jelly. I eased myself down onto the bed. Now that I was reasonably sure I wasn't about to get strangled by a maniac in neon green, I took a few deep breaths. I felt my heart rate slow down enough for me to ask two of the thousand questions swirling in my brain. "Shouldn't you be in heaven with a harp or something? What are you doing here?"

"I don't know!" The ghost paced the room, again walking

right through trophies and knickknacks as though they didn't exist—or as if *he* didn't.

I whimpered unintentionally and scooted back against the wall. Family or not, this was *weird*. But I had to admit . . . it was also kind of cool. All this time I had been wishing I had gotten to know my abuelo more, and now here he was in the flesh. Well, maybe not in the *flesh*, but close enough.

"What do you remember?" I asked.

"There was a tunnel of light, just like everybody always says, and at the end of it, the most glorious party you've ever seen! And it was all for me! I'm sure of it! But then I was ambushed by my former bandmate . . . uh . . . Ernesto, and he stole my dog and sent me back here."

He turned and stretched out a hand from across the room. I cringed but managed to keep from breaking anything else.

"I'm stuck here," he went on. "I can't leave this house—believe me, I've tried—and nobody can see me. Except you, my boy!" He reached for me then, like he was trying to grab my shoulders. I scrambled away from him, scared to let his transparent fingers get any closer. I had no idea what it would feel like to get hugged by a ghost, and I was in no hurry to find out.

"Th-that's awful," I stammered, just because it felt like I ought to say something while I dodged his embrace.

He let his arms drop. "It gets worse," he replied.

As he paced, the rhinestones on the loose-fitting pants

glittered in the overhead lights. Was that what Abuelo had been wearing when he died, or is that what they forced you to wear in ghost limbo? Maybe people lost their fashion sense when they died?

"He had the nerve to tell me I wasn't a good person! Can you believe that?"

"Well, I don't really—"

"That's right, nieto. I wasn't just good. I was great!" he cried, twirling his index finger up into the air. "But before that traitor sent me back, he told me I had unfinished business here. I have to figure out what it is and resolve it by New Year's so I can prove I'm not so bad. Only then I'll be allowed in and can make my big entrance at the afterlife party already. But if I can't . . . I'll be trapped here for good."

My mouth went dry. This was too big a problem for me to solve.

"I've gotta tell my parents," I said, leaping up from the bed. "They'll know what to do."

"Benny, stop!" he shouted as I ran out the door. "They won't be able to see me! Wait!"

I ran downstairs to the master suite and burst through the fancy French doors. Inside, Mami and Papi were sorting through a pile of clothes that was bigger than I was. Guayaberas, suits, hats, tuxedos—now I knew why Abuelo needed a whole *suite*.

"¿Qué pasa, Benny?" Mami asked. "Is everything okay?"

I tried to talk, but I was out of breath from sprinting through this mansion. I gasped for air, pivoting back and forth between my mother and my father.

"Look . . . Abuelo . . . my room."

That's when I noticed the two big garbage bags at the foot of the bed, both overflowing with shirts and pants.

From behind me, I heard Abuelo cry out, "*My clothes! Are they throwing them away? But why? That's high-end stuff! Félix could use some designer threads!*"

Papi stood and walked toward us. Did he see Abuelo? If anybody should be able to see him, it would be his own son. Papi reached out and . . . took the mannequin arm from me. I blinked. I had forgotten I was holding it.

Papi tsked. "I thought we agreed you wouldn't touch anything else. Why are you carrying this arm around?"

I opened my mouth to explain, but Mami's shriek interrupted me.

She held up an ugly gold-colored shirt, decked out in colorful plastic sequins. "What was Ignacio *thinking*?"

"What was I thinking?" Abuelo repeated. "¿Qué te crees tú? That was my lucky shirt!"

Papi shook his head as he laid the mannequin arm aside and grabbed the shirt. "If there was anything Ignacio loved, it was being noticed. Let's put it in the donation bag."

"¿Qué?" came Abuelo's outraged voice from behind me.

"You can't donate that!" I blurted out. "That was Abuelo's lucky shirt!"

My parents both stared at me.

"And you would know that how?" Papi asked.

"Um, I mean, *look* at it! A shirt like that *has* to be lucky! Why else would you wear it?"

Papi shrugged and tossed it to me. "All right, if you like it so much, you can have it."

Just as I caught the heinous shirt, the doorbell rang.

"That must be the pizza!" Papi grabbed his wallet and hurried out of the room, Abuelo's ghost disappearing a split second before Papi would have walked through him.

Trying to control my breathing, I tied the shirt's long sleeves around my waist and followed my parents, keeping my eyes peeled the whole time for Abuelo. Where could he have gone?

Cristina and Manny were already waiting in the foyer, and we helped Papi carry the pizza boxes and sodas into the living room. Cristina cleared space on the coffee table, and I passed out paper plates while our parents collapsed onto the couch.

"We'll have to order in for a while," Mami said. "Until we can unpack all our cooking stuff. A house this big, I thought for sure it would have an impressive kitchen, but there're just two bowls, two plates, a pair of cups . . . it's like he never had anybody join him for a meal except Guillermo."

I chewed on my slice as she talked, thinking about

everything that had just happened. Had I really seen a ghost, and was he gone now? Sitting here eating pizza with my family, I suddenly thought the whole thing seemed ridiculous. I couldn't have seen a ghost! Could I have imagined something that weird, though? It *was* a pretty long trip. And I was already sleepy and tired when we got here. It was so hot outside, maybe the sun fried my brain.

Yeah, I had to have imagined it, I thought.

But then I caught a glimpse of motion on the stairs. Abuelo sat staring at us all like some sad kid who didn't get invited to the big birthday party. When he saw me look his way, he waved.

Before I could catch myself, I yelped.

"What's wrong?" Manny asked.

I drew a breath to ask him if he could see Abuelo—maybe it was a kid thing, and that was why Guillermo and my parents couldn't see him. But no. Cristina was sitting right next to me, and she didn't seem to see anything either.

"Um, just jumpy, I guess. It's such a big house."

"Manny," Mami said, "if you don't want the peppers, leave them on your plate. Don't pile them up on the coffee table."

" 'This is between me and the vegetable!' " he said, quoting *Little Shop of Horrors* in that Actor voice he used when he was in character, as though he were projecting to the back row of an auditorium.

"Are you nervous about school tomorrow?" Papi asked me.

Cristina popped one of Manny's discarded green peppers into her mouth.

"'You ate the only thing I ever loved!'" Manny exclaimed.

"You know what I'm going to love?" Cristina said, standing up with a slice in her hand. She pirouetted past the alligator. "Dancing circles around everybody at that school."

"'We're not talking about one hungry plant here,'" Manny said. "'We're talking about world conquest.'"

Abuelo left his perch on the stairs and mirrored Cristina's moves, jeté-ing away next to her. The rhinestones on his jacket twinkled with every movement.

"Stop that!" I barked.

"I will not!" Manny said. "Preparation is an important part of my craft. The only way I'll be ready to nail the monologue and song tomorrow is if I get into character early. In fact, please stop calling me Manny. My name is Seymour."

"You see, Benny?" Abuelo spun around Cristina as if he were her invisible partner. "Only you can see me."

"I can't believe this," I said.

"I would think you'd be used to them by now," Papi replied.

"Believe it!" Abuelo exclaimed. "Here! I'll prove it!"

He left Cristina's side and marched around the coffee table, whistling the "Himno Nacional Cubano." It turned out Abuelo was one of those people with the ear-piercingly loud whistles.

I covered my ears, which prompted Manny to shout his lines louder. For his part, Abuelo started playing an imaginary trumpet, marching around as though it were half-time at a football game.

SOMEHOW, I GOT through dinner without my head exploding. I looked around the coffee table now. Mami and Papi were talking about the classes they'd be teaching. Cristina was still leaping and kicking about the room while Manny argued with an invisible flower-shop owner. Though I still had no idea what to do about Abuelo, watching them all get lost in their talents brought me right back to my first worry: How in the world was I going to survive at a performing arts school? I only had a few hours left until school started, and I was no closer to figuring out what my talent would be than when I first discovered Abuelo's ghost in my room.

I shoved the last piece of crust into my mouth, chewed, and swallowed. "Can I be excused?"

I had to raise my voice to be heard over all the separate performances.

Papi checked his watch. "Oh! Sure. It's late. And we all have an early start tomorrow."

I said good night and hurried upstairs before I could accidentally say anything that might seem weird.

I mean, weirder than everything else that was going on.

I wasn't actually sleepy, though; I just wanted space to think. So up in my room I opened the balcony door and stood in the frame, staring out at my new . . . well, not neighborhood, because you needed to be able to see neighbors to call it a neighborhood. My new surroundings.

The night felt different here in Florida than in Los Angeles. Nights were warm there too, but here the air was humid and thick, pressing against my skin as if it were trying to give me a hug. A hint of a breeze wafted in too—the promise of rain.

Behind me a quiet voice said, "I tried to tell you."

I managed not to jump, though maybe I flinched a little. I turned around. "They really can't see or hear you."

Abuelo shook his head. "I haven't been able to communicate with anybody since I died. Not even Iggy 2, though he could just be ignoring me. He *was* always a bit standoffish."

It made me sad to hear Abuelo say this. I often felt invisible. But he was invisible for real. And for some reason, *I*, the unremarkable Ramírez, was the only one who could see him.

Oh no—what if *this* was my talent? Speaking to the dead. I couldn't think of anything more depressing. It definitely wouldn't win me any popularity points at school. But could there be a silver lining to it? "Maybe it's my job to help you," I offered.

Abuelo scoffed. "The great Ignacio Ramírez, needing

help from a boy? That doesn't make any—" His eyes widened. "Wait! I've got it! Maybe I'm supposed to prove I'm worthy of the afterlife . . . by helping *you*!" He pointed a gnarled finger at me, nearly poking me in the forehead. "Tell me, boy! Tell me your problems, and I will solve them. I have always succeeded at everything I've tried. What do you need?"

I blinked. I guess that made as much sense as my idea. Maybe more. I perked up, suddenly relieved. If he was right, that meant my talent didn't have anything to do with speaking to the dead. Maybe Abuelo was here to help me. Perhaps with a little guidance from the dearly departed—well, *nearly* departed, anyway—I wouldn't have to be the hopeless Ramírez after all. "Could you help me be as great as you at something?"

"Eh?" He frowned. "Well, let's not get ahead of ourselves. No one can be quite as great as *me*. But I'll try to get you close. Ramírezes don't usually need any help being at least a little great, though. So tell me, mi nieto, what's the problem?"

I closed the balcony door. I knew it would sound silly to say that my problem was being ordinary. That isn't usually a problem. But it sure feels like one when you're in an extraordinary family, and you're about to go to a school for extraordinary kids.

"I'm nervous about school tomorrow. It's a magnet school for talented kids, and I don't have any talent at all. Cristina and Manny will fit right in, but I won't belong."

Abuelo stiffened. "My boy, we share the same blood. How dare you say you are not talented! I am a winner, and though you aren't one now, you will be too!"

Did my abuelo just call me a loser? "Um, okay. What do I do?"

He pointed toward the shirt still hanging around my waist. "For starters, wear that to school tomorrow. I promise you; all the kids will love it!"

I ran a hand through my hair. I probably shouldn't be basing my wardrobe on this totally-fictional-definitely-not-real ghost in my head. I mean, the shirt may have been one of a kind, but not in a good way. I doubted it would help me make a great first impression with the kids at school. But for a figment of my imagination, Abuelo was pretty convincing.

"Okay, I guess," I said, eyeing the shirt uncertainly.

Abuelo clapped his hands together. "Perfect! Second, we should get to know each other!"

Finally! I had always wanted an abuelo who cared about me and wanted to know me. "Cool! Well, I like streaming videos, and playing—"

"Hush, we don't have time for that. There is so much you must learn about the incredible Ignacio Ramírez, if you are going to be a winner like me! Sit down, and I'll tell you everything!"

CHAPTER THREE

In the morning, while Papi drove us all to school, I leaned my head against the window, watching unfamiliar landmarks whiz past and blinking sleep out of my eyes. I had stayed up way too late, but Abuelo's stories were amazing. He had seen and experienced so much, from finding his love of music in church choir to having a monster hit and meeting celebrities around the world. Just hearing about his exciting life made me feel like mine was exciting too. I had drifted off somewhere in the middle of Abuelo's third world tour. When I woke up, he was gone, having disappeared to wherever ghosts go when they aren't haunting their grandkids.

I realized with dread that in all that talking, he hadn't actually gotten around to telling me how I should handle school today. On the upside, I was too sleepy to feel nervous, so I guess it had kind of worked. *Oh well,* I thought. *I'll just keep my head down. If I can't stand out, at least I can blend in.*

My face heated up a bit at the thought. Blending in hadn't been Abuelo's plan for me, but when I stepped out of my room in Abuelo's sequined lucky shirt, Cristina's and Manny's stares were enough to make me lose my nerve and want to leave the shirt behind.

"*That's* what you're wearing?" Cristina asked.

I gulped, trying to remember how Abuelo had made wearing the shirt seem like a great idea. "Yeah. It was Abuelo's, and I like it. So?"

"So . . . ," Manny said cautiously. "You know we're going to school, not performing a magic show in Las Vegas, right?"

Cristina giggled. When I shot her a glare, she hurried to say, "Sorry, Benny! But you have to admit . . . it's a little . . ."

"Butt ugly?" Manny blurted. "Worse than Papi's Christmas sweater with the light-up reindeer on the front?"

Cristina elbowed Manny and flashed him a scolding look. "I was going to say *bold*. But, hey, if you're sure, Benny, I say go ahead and rock it."

I gave Cristina a grateful smile. "Thanks."

"Sure," she said, turning toward the stairs. "Just warn us next time to put on sunglasses first. Pretty sure it isn't good for our eyes to look directly at it."

"Ha ha. Real funny," I mumbled as I ducked back into

my room to snatch a plain gray hoodie—just in case—then followed them downstairs.

Mami and Papi were waiting by the door. When they saw me, they exchanged a look—part horror, part amusement—and Mami opened her mouth to say something, but Cristina stopped her. She held up a hand and said, "Don't bother. We already tried."

No one brought the shirt up on the drive. They all seemed too focused on their own plans to make a first impression.

Manny—er, *Seymour*—kept muttering lines to himself, trying to decide what sounded best. "'What do you want from me—*blood*? What do you *want* from me—blood? What do you want from *me*—blood?'" The really cool thing was that the same words *did* seem to mean something different each time he said them.

Cristina had her earbuds in, listening to the music she planned to dance to today. As we rounded bends in the road, she swayed slightly in her seat, mentally rehearsing her routine, small movements standing in for the big swoops and leaps she would take on the dance floor. They both came across so confident and carefree.

At least, right up until Papi turned in to the school's driveway.

Cristina pulled out one of the earbuds. "Wait—*that's* the school? This place is a hole!" she said, gesturing with disgust.

I looked at the building.

"What's wrong with it?" I asked.

"It's tiny! It can't be big enough to have a proper dance studio. They probably aren't even affiliated with a talent agency!"

I tried to see it through her eyes. Twin pine trees towered over a two-story brick building, while single-story structures stood on either side. Okay, the place was small. The whole property could probably fit inside the parking lot of our old school. But it had a homier feel. The windows were made of actual glass, not metal slats, and the grounds were filled with trees and grassy spaces and benches—like a place you might enjoy spending time in, instead of a juvenile detention center.

"It's bigger inside than it appears," said Mami. "Your father and I took a virtual tour when we were enrolling you three. It's cozy!"

"*Cozy* is code for *small*," Cristina sulked.

"Ya, Cristina," Mami said with a sigh.

I checked on Manny, to see if he was equally dismayed. But he didn't say anything. He just stared past me, out the window, his eyes wide. Was he still being Seymour? Or was Manny freaking out?

Somebody on the sidewalk skated by, laughing loudly and nearly sideswiping us. Manny flinched, as though, somehow, he could get hurt in the middle of the backseat of an SUV.

"'Guy sure looks like plant food to me,'" Manny muttered.

I took a breath, feeling oddly better. I didn't *want* my brother and sister to be unhappy, but . . . at least I wasn't alone in being a bit unsure about all this.

Papi turned in to a fenced-in lot, found a space, and cut off the engine. "All right, Ramírez family. Let's do this!"

We entered through a side door, my gut clenching with every step.

A round woman with red hair pulled into a bun met us at the door. "Felix! Luisa! Welcome!" She pronounced my father's name FEEL-ix, instead of FEH-leex. She waved as she called out, directing even more attention our way. "And these must be the kids!"

My face burned. *No. I'm just a stranger who happens to be walking in at the same time as the new teachers. Please, nobody notice me.* But as I watched her gaze sweep right past Manny and Cristina to land squarely on my "lucky" shirt, and I saw her eyes widen, I knew my chances of blending in were slim to none.

"I'm Mrs. Palmer," she went on after a moment. "Why don't the three of you come with me, and I'll help you get set up while your parents go to the faculty orientation breakfast."

I would rather have run home. But I chose the path of least resistance, said goodbye to Mami and Papi, and followed Mrs. Palmer in, along with Manny and Cristina. She led us through a crazy winding corridor, past a steady stream of other students. After I caught one kid looking at my shirt and then dramatically shielding his face and crying, "My eyes! My eeeeeyes!" I slipped on my hoodie and zipped it up to my neck. We trailed behind Mrs. Palmer into a room separated from a lobby full of parents and kids by a row of interior windows.

"I've got your schedules right here on my desk," she said. "Except for one. Which one of you is Benny?"

I cleared my throat. "That's me."

She handed printouts to Manny and Cristina, then walked around the desk to sit before her computer. "I noticed that you don't have a talent selected yet. You'll need to choose an art to go with your academic courses." She hit a few keys and pulled up my file. "Benicio Ignacio Ramírez," she read. She turned to me with a gleam in her eye. "Ignacio . . . is that after your grandfather?"

I puffed out my chest a little. "Yes, ma'am."

"Does that mean you can play the trumpet like he did?" she asked, her eyebrows raised hopefully.

At that, Manny and Cristina choked back laughter. "Oh, definitely. His trumpet-playing is legendary!" Cristina said with a nearly straight face.

Manny, never one to miss an acting opportunity, added, "His cover of 'Somewhere Over the Rainbow' would make you cry." He pretended to be overcome with emotion as he wiped a nonexistent tear from the corner of his eye.

I scowled, already making plans to get back at them later.

The thing is, the sarcasm sailed right over Mrs. Palmer's head.

"Wonderful!" Mrs. Palmer chirped. "That's settled, then! You'll join the band."

My eyes bulged. "Wait, what? No. But I—"

"I know, you're worried the rest of the children won't be at your level. But I assure you, our program only admits the best. And you will be our crown jewel!"

I stared at Manny and Cristina helplessly, but they seemed just as stunned.

She tapped some keys and handed me a printout. My eyes glazed as I read it. Band was first period.

And second.

"All our arts are double-blocked here," she said, as if reading my mind. "After all, it's kind of our thing."

"Great," I mumbled.

She sent the three of us on our way. Halfway down the hall, Cristina whispered, "But you can't—"

"I know," I whispered back.

"I mean, you've never even held a—"

"I know!" I interrupted Manny. "Remind me later to thank you for that moving performance back there." I glared at my siblings, who at least had the decency to look sorry. We parted ways and I started walking toward the band room, located at the back of the campus.

As I walked, I thought. Mostly about how I was going to survive this. And then something occurred to me: Maybe my abuelo appeared to me the night before for a reason! Even if he hadn't *exactly* explained how I was supposed to succeed in this school, he understood the problem, right? I didn't totally understand how the ghost thing worked, but maybe I'd absorbed some of his Ramírez magic just from being so close to his spirit. If a laugh can be infectious, maybe talent could be too, and I'd be able to play the trumpet like he played the trumpet.

It wasn't much, but it was the only hope I had.

CHAPTER FOUR

When I knocked on the band-room door, I was greeted by the teacher, Mr. Edwards, a short man with long hair, a beard, and a big smile. He shook my hand and said, "Welcome to SMPAS." He said it like a word. *Sim-pass.* "Mrs. Palmer called ahead to let me know you were coming. I have to say, this is quite an honor to have a Ramírez prodigy in my class. Come in, come in!"

"Er, thanks," I croaked as I entered the well-insulated chamber.

Then he turned to the class and said, "Everyone, say hello to our newest member, Benny Ignacio Ramírez." The others, already setting up music stands and opening instrument cases, all stopped to wave at me and say hi. A few whispered to each other while keeping their eyes on me, as if they were already starstruck. *That's right, I've got the talent of Ignacio Ramírez in my very lungs!* I thought. *Or . . . in the shirt? Ay, I just hope I have it somewhere.*

After taking attendance, Mr. Edwards asked, "Benny, did you bring your trumpet?"

"I don't have—" I caught myself. "I don't have it here. I didn't realize I'd get to play it today!"

He nodded slowly, and directed me to the instrument storage room, where I found a single beat-up trumpet that smelled like mildew. Then he brought me over to the trumpet section of the class. "Harold, would you mind moving to the back?" he said to the boy in the first chair. "It's just for today. Until Benny gets acquainted with how we do things here. You can play the second trumpet part, and Benny can split first trumpet with DeSean."

Harold looked put out, but he quietly picked up his instrument and trumpet stand and moved awkwardly to the last row. Suddenly I was sitting right up front, where I could feel everyone's eyes on my neck. If Ignacio was with me, I hoped he felt less scared than I did.

"Great. Let's get started." Mr. Edwards took his position behind a music stand in the front of the room and lifted his baton. "Easy stuff first: let's hear a concert B-flat scale, whole notes."

I had no idea what Mr. Edwards had just said. My entire

mouth felt dry as sand as I lifted the trumpet to my lips, hoping the Ignacio magic would take over any minute. All I had to do was blow into one end and press some keys, try to follow everyone else's lead.

I blew as hard as I could and pressed random buttons with my fingers.

It was official. My abuelo was *not* possessing any part of me. The lucky shirt was a fail too. The belches and honks that came out *were* otherworldly, but not in a good way. More like a demon elephant that had been surprised and was showing its displeasure.

Mr. Edwards winced and waved his arms. "Stop! What was that?" he demanded. "Sounds like some of you have not been practicing. Perhaps we should have Mr. Ramírez play the scale by himself to remind you all what it should sound like."

I nearly fell out of my chair. "M-m-me?" I stammered.

"Who better?" said Mr. Edwards. He raised his baton again and nodded at me.

I gulped. This wasn't going to be pretty. *Come on, Ignacio!* I lifted the trumpet to my lips again and tried to channel Abuelo. In one of his stories the night before, he'd made it sound so easy—like the first time he'd picked up a trumpet, it was as if he were discovering a long-lost limb. *I just let the trumpet tell me what to do,* he'd said. I tried to do the same, hoping that it was the key to getting *music* to come out.

I took a deep breath and then forced air out of my lungs as if I were trying to blow up a balloon, and I put down one finger, then two, then three. The sounds coming out weren't any more pleasing than before, but at least they sounded like different notes. Still, there was no denying it now: I was no Ignacio Ramírez. The nice thing about having the instrument so close to my face was, though I heard my classmates giggling, I couldn't *see* them.

I reached the top of my improvised scale and was about to head back down when Mr. Edwards coughed and said, "Okay! That's enough. Thank you!"

"Are you sure?"

"Quite sure! Um . . . tell you what. I just realized our triangle player is missing today." He reached into a cabinet and pulled out a silver triangle with a small metal rod. He handed them both to me and said, "Why don't you switch places with Harold and strike the triangle whenever I give you the nod, okay?"

I clutched the triangle and made my way to the back row, passing Harold, who seemed vindicated on his way up front.

From my new seat I could see several of the other students giving one another puzzled looks. Of course they were confused. They'd all auditioned to get here, so they assumed I had too. They hadn't put it together yet that I was really just a "kid of faculty" admission masquerading as a musical prodigy. No way would I have passed an audition with my screechy trumpet-playing. They clearly took music very seriously; it had been silly to think I could fake my way through it. My face burned. There was nothing I could do but pretend I was oblivious.

After class, Mr. Edwards asked me to stay behind. Once all the other kids had left, he took a seat across from me, took off his glasses, and rubbed the bridge of his nose. "Tell me honestly, kiddo. Have you ever played the trumpet before?"

I knew I should probably come clean now, but it was too humiliating. So I dug the hole I was in a little deeper. "It's just been a long time," I said. "And I'm not used to playing someone else's trumpet."

Mr. Edwards nodded knowingly, as if that made all the sense in the world. "Of course," he said. "Mrs. Palmer informed me that you just moved here from California. I'm sure you haven't had much time to play. And between you and me, I don't like using borrowed instruments either. So tomorrow feel free to bring in your own trumpet and we'll try again, shall we?"

I nodded numbly. What had I gotten myself into? But then I remembered that I could track down my trumpet-playing poltergeist tonight—and remind him that he'd *already* sworn to help me. I could only hope his powers included turning me into an expert trumpet player in less than twenty-four hours. "Yeah, I guess that might work."

Mr. Edwards patted me on the back and wrote me a pass to math class. All through math and language arts, I wondered who in the room had heard my performance, or heard *about* it. I swore I could hear snickering now and then, and I had the sinking feeling it was about me. So I kept my eyes down and tried to avoid doing anything (else) to stand out.

At last, lunchtime came. *Finally,* I thought. *Something I'm good at.*

I searched for Cristina and Manny but soon realized they weren't there. They must've been scheduled for different lunch periods. That meant I was on my own.

I waited in line, got a tray of slop with mashed potatoes, gravy, and green beans, and walked around, searching for someplace to sit. But everywhere I looked, the tables were full—drama kids like Manny at one table, acting out scenes; dance students like Cristina comparing ballet slippers; even art kids with splotches of paint on their clothes.

The only spot I found open was at a table where a girl with unnaturally pale skin and pitch-black hair sat by herself, jotting something into a notebook.

Was she the local unpopular kid? Would sitting beside her make me unpopular too?

Whatever. I was already not going to be popular, and if I didn't eat soon, lunch would be over, and I'd be unpopular *and* hungry.

"Hi," I said, just because it felt weird to plant myself at somebody else's table and not say anything.

The girl glanced up, staring for a moment as though waiting for me to say something else, and then returned to her notebook.

I shrugged and cut off a corner of mystery meat—which might have been turkey, or chicken, or tofu. I could see there were a few fresh herbs thrown on top of the soggy mess. Clearly, somebody had *tried* with this, but it hadn't been enough to save the salty meatlike substance.

"I see even in artsy magnet schools, cafeteria food is still gross," I said. "It's nice to know some things never change."

"My mom is the cook," Goth girl said, her attention still on her notebook.

My eyes widened. Of *course* she was.

"I—I'm so sorry," I stammered. "I shouldn't have said that out loud!"

She shrugged. "Don't be sorry," she said, finally looking at me and talking *at the same time.* "I agree with you. *She* agrees with you. She used to teach home economics before budget cuts made them eliminate the program. She only took this job to stay at my school. But she knows how to make good food. She'd be doing that if she could. She loves coming up with recipes. But they only have the budget to buy processed stuff and heat it up, you know? Most of the students here bring their own lunch."

I nodded. "Maybe I'll do that tomorrow. What's your name?"

She straightened and held out a hand. "Andrea Wade, future playwright."

My heart sank a little. When she said her mom was the cook, I'd started to hope maybe I'd found another staff-kid no-talent like myself, but even *she* was an artist.

I shook her hand. "I'm Benny. Future, uh, something. What kind of plays do you write?"

She scooted over to my end of the table, sitting across from me. "I like to write about ghosts and supernatural stuff. That's why I usually end up sitting alone. The other people here aren't into that. Wanna see?"

I felt my scalp tingle at the mention of ghosts. Did I have a story for her—if I were stupid enough to go telling it.

She must have mistaken my little chill for a shudder, or for shaking my head, because her eyes fell. "Sorry," she said. "I know you didn't sit here on purpose. I'll leave you alone."

"No!" I hurried to say. "That wasn't it! I'd love to see what you write!"

She grinned. "You're easy to manipulate. I like you!"

She came around to my side of the table and sat next to me. "Here's what I'm currently working on," she said, flipping back several pages in her notebook. "It's called *The Haunted Lunchroom*."

She pointed at a line near the top. "Why don't you read the part of Jason? You'll be a seventh grader being haunted by a possessed fish stick."

"Um, okay." I cleared my throat. *"Jason enters stage left—"*

"You don't read that part. You read the stuff that comes after the name."

"Sorry, yeah. Okay, um, *Help me, Francine*—" I looked up from the script. "Is that you?"

"Yes." She nodded. "I mean, I'll play Francine. She's a ghost hunter."

"Okay. *Help me, Francine. I think this fish stick is possessed.*"

"*Don't worry, Jason. I've got ghost-proof shrink-wrap. Hah! Gotcha! Now this demon is gonna fry!*"

"*Are you sending it to the underworld?*"

"*No, to the kitchen! This fish stick is haunting you because it has unfinished business. Think for a moment—have you ever eaten tuna salad?*"

"*Yes, but—*"

"*Monster! You don't deserve to be rescued!*"

"Huh?" I said, looking up from the script and pointing at the line. "What does Francine mean by that?"

Andrea huffed. "The fish is clearly after you for chomping his tuna friends!"

I snorted. This stuff was over the top, but it was kind of funny. "Sorry," I said. "Didn't mean to break character. I'm not really an actor."

"That's okay," Andrea said, grinning. "Neither am I."

"I liked the part about the fish stick having unfinished business." I thought about Abuelo, and his theory that *I* was his unfinished business. "Where did you get that from?"

"Oh, everybody knows. All ghosts have unfinished business."

I felt the smile leave my face. "You know a lot about ghosts?"

She shrugged. "Kind of." She glanced out of the corner of her eye, as though waiting for me to say something mean. When I didn't say anything, she went on. "My house is haunted."

I gasped. "Really?"

"We live in a really old house in Coconut Grove," she said. "I can totally sense when a ghost is present."

My mouth dried up. Was it possible I wasn't the only one with a ghost grandpa? Cristina and Manny hadn't been able to see Abuelo, but maybe Andrea would! Better yet, maybe she could help me figure out why Abuelo was still in Miami, Florida, instead of the Great Beyond.

"Want to come over after school?" I blurted out. "My brother's an actor. We could all act out the rest of your play."

Andrea gave me a surprised smile, like she wasn't used to getting invited anywhere. "I'll have to ask my mom, but if she says yes, sure! As long as I still get to play Francine. I'm a born ghost hunter."

I didn't exactly need a ghost hunter—I'd found Abuelo just fine on my own, after all. But I'd take whatever help—and friends—I could get.

CHAPTER FIVE

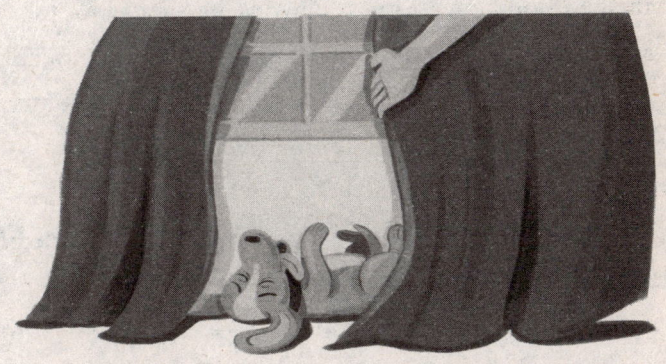

After school, I met Andrea by the service door behind the cafeteria. Once she had her mom's permission to come over, we hurried to the teacher parking lot. I took in Andrea's appearance: she wore a black skirt and a long-sleeve shirt with a cartoon rabbit on it, which looked normal enough unless you considered that the rabbit was wearing a spiky collar and had a black eye and bandages on it. The fact that anybody would wear a long-sleeve shirt in this Miami heat blew my mind. Of course, I still had on the hoodie zipped up to my neck to hide the glittery gold shirt, so who was I to talk? But I was a little nervous about how my family would react to my new friend all the same.

It wouldn't be nice to call Andrea *weird,* but she was . . . quirky.

Cristina was waiting beside the SUV when we got there, but she stood alone. I guess new teachers had a lot to attend to after the first day of school, and Manny was probably off being Manny somewhere. Knowing him, he had an audience of fans oohing and aahing over his total transformation into his latest character.

"Hey, Cristina," I said. "How's it going?" I braced for a barrage of questions about who Andrea was.

She blinked at me, as though it took her a moment to figure out who *I* was. "They hated me, Benny. They thought I was terrible."

My eyes widened. Cristina was very much not terrible. "What? Somebody said that?"

"Well, no, but I danced my routine, and nobody applauded."

Andrea frowned. "Was this a performance or a class?"

Cristina stared at her, as though noticing her for the first time, and then turned to me, an eyebrow raised.

"Um, Cristina, this is Andrea. She's a playwright."

"Hey," Cristina said, giving her a half-hearted wave and taking her appearance in stride. Andrea waved back, then Cristina went on. "It doesn't matter. I mean, it doesn't usually matter if it's a performance or a class. I don't get nervous for either one, so it's all the same to me. And I always get applause. *Always.* Today? Nothing. Crickets."

"But did anybody say you were bad?" Andrea persisted.

Cristina glanced away. "The teacher."

I blinked. "The teacher said you were terrible?" What kind of arts school was this?

She sighed. "Basically."

I gave her the side-eye. "*Basically?* What were her actual words?"

"She listed all the things I'd done wrong!"

"Well, I mean, that's kind of what teachers do."

"That's not all. She said . . . she said . . ." Cristina swallowed. "She said I needed to work on my technique. She said I, Cristina Ramírez, had poor technique! Can you believe that?"

"I—"

"And it gets worse!"

"Worse?"

She nodded and sniffed. "There's a production of *The Nutcracker* coming up, and when I said I was willing to do it, the teacher told me I needed to *audition*. And there's this other girl—Sarah—she was so mean! She thinks she's so great." Cristina's voice wavered. "She thinks she's better than me. Do you think she's better than me?"

I held up my hands, trying to slow the emotion train down. "Um, no? I don't know." I shot Andrea a desperate look, but she shrugged and stayed quiet. "You're probably just rusty from all that time in the car. Once you get some practice, maybe you'll dance better."

Cristina's lip trembled. "So you *do* think I'm a terrible dancer!"

"What? No, I didn't mean . . . That's not what I . . ." Being the reassuring one wasn't my strong suit. But in my defense, Cristina usually didn't need reassuring.

I glanced across the parking lot, as though I might see a sign somewhere with the right words to say. Instead, I saw Manny coming toward us. "Oh look, here's Manny," I blurted.

When he joined us, I gestured at our guest. "Hey, this is Andrea. She writes plays. I thought you might help us run through scenes." I turned toward Andrea. "This is my brother, Manny—um, sorry, no. Right now, he's Seymour, uh . . ." I struggled to remember the last name of the character from *Little Shop*.

"Manny's fine," he said, the words coming out in a monotone.

I peered at him. His arms hung limply at his sides, and his chin practically touched his chest. "Hey," I asked, "are you okay?"

He shrugged. "Yup. I'm great."

Something in the way he spoke told me that was definitely not true. I heard the slightest tremble in his voice. Most people wouldn't have even noticed it, but I knew my brother. Something was wrong. Did he have as rotten a day as Cristina had? I started to ask, but just then, our parents arrived.

"Mami, Papi, this is Andrea. Her mom works at the

school. I told her she could come over. Is that okay? Her mom already said yes."

Mami glanced at Cristina, and then at Papi, one eyebrow up and a slight smile on her lips. Papi met her gaze and smiled back, like they were talking telepathically. I wasn't sure what was going on, but I didn't like it. It felt a little like somebody had told a joke and everybody got it except me.

"Sure, sweetie. It's so nice to meet you, Andrea. I'm glad Benny is already making friends at his new school!" Glancing around at the rest of the group, she asked, "How did everybody else's day go?"

Manny and Cristina mumbled vague replies as we all squeezed into the backseat. Cristina had been begging our parents to get a minivan or an SUV with three rows of seats for as long as I could remember—maybe if we all started bringing friends home from school, we could get them to listen. As it was, we were crammed in so tightly that my ribs felt like they were getting crushed. I didn't *think* it was possible to get squeezed into pulp from being packed into the car like garlic in a press, but I wasn't ruling it out either.

The whole ride, my parents kept trying to get us talking about our day—as if any of us could breathe well enough to talk. I didn't exactly want to relive getting slotted into band class and my disastrous trumpet-playing. Cristina had needed little prodding to tell *me* how rotten her day had been, but now she had nothing to say. And I didn't know yet what was wrong with Manny, but he wasn't talking either.

I'd fully expected to struggle to fit in, but Cristina and Manny should have been naturals here.

When nobody else spoke up, Andrea jumped in to fill the silence. "Well, I'm excited that we've finally got a playwriting class this year. Creative writing was fine, but it was all short stories about cute dogs and bad friends. BO-RING. I'm looking forward to joining the poetry club, though. You should join it with me, Benny!"

"Oh, I—I don't know. I'm not much of a poet," I said.

Andrea shrugged. "Me neither, but so many poems are about ghosts and goblins and spooky things. I just feel like it will be perfect for me, you know? Might even give me ideas for future plays. Like there's this one poem where a guy obsesses about his dead wife and is haunted by a creepy raven? Could be fun to write about a long-lost relative reaching out from beyond the grave—or maybe a zombie owl!" She wiggled her fingers and mimicked a ghostly "ooOOOoo."

I cringed, expecting somebody to question why anyone would be that interested in ghosts and lost relatives and zombified birds of prey, but nobody seemed to mind.

"Anyway, Manny," she went on, "it would be cool if the playwriting class and the acting kids worked together. I'm always trying to get actors to do my plays."

Manny grunted noncommittally.

"I'll tell you what, Manny," Papi said. "Those drama kids are really something! So close-knit! You're going to have a great time with them!"

"Yeah, sure," Manny mumbled, his voice a little husky. "I just need to study my lines. The first production of the year is gonna be *Alice in Wonderland,* and I have a lot to memorize for the auditions."

"I love how focused you are," Papi said. "You—and all the drama kids—really care about this. So many of the adult actors I've worked with just took for granted how amazing it was to get to do this stuff. I'm so excited to work with young people like you and your friends."

Manny looked out the window. "Uh-huh."

"It's like going back to where it all started for me. I can't wait. After you've had time to study your part, let me know if you want somebody to run lines with you."

Manny's eyes widened a little at that. "You mean . . . you?"

"¡Claro!" Papi said. "Who better? It'll be fun!"

Manny let out a stunned "Okay. Thanks." Papi had never had time to do things like run lines with him before. I could tell that was going to take almost as much getting used to as moving to Miami.

"You know," Andrea said, "I'm a playwright, not an actor, but I have to know my scripts backward and forward, to make sure everything connects like it should. Something I find helpful is to doodle in the margins. Like, if I have a line about ghost zombies eating your brains, I draw a little picture of that next to the line. Then when I'm trying to memorize the script, I think of the drawing, and it helps me remember the words on the page too."

I tensed up, expecting Manny to be offended. Andrea didn't understand how talented everybody else in my family was. She had met me, the new kid who couldn't find a place to sit in the cafeteria after his disastrous trumpet audition, and probably thought we were all in the same boat. She didn't realize the last thing in the world Manny needed was tips on learning a part.

But Manny just turned to her and said, "That's good advice. Thanks."

I scanned his face, waiting for him to follow that up with a bit of sarcasm, but he seemed sincere.

The rest of the drive passed silently, until we pulled into the gate to our house—well, technically *Abuelo's* house, since he was still there.

Andrea stared out the window. "You live *here*?"

I imagined how this must look through her eyes. Suddenly I felt self-conscious taking in our new house—correction, *mansion*. It wasn't exactly a typical place to live. More like something you'd see in a movie about a wealthy globe-hopping superspy. I wasn't sure what it made her think about us, or how to explain that we were just a normal family (mostly), so I stayed quiet. But she was glued to the window, so I guess it was okay that I had no words.

As soon as we parked and walked through the front door, Manny and Cristina stomped off to their rooms with barely more than a *See ya later*.

I turned to Andrea and frowned. "I'm sorry. I'd hoped Manny at least would read lines with us, but . . ."

She shrugged. "It's okay. Honestly, I'm used to reading all the parts by myself anyway." She bit her lip, as though she had just admitted something she hadn't intended to. "We can read them with just the two of us, the way we were doing at lunch." She spun a bit, taking in the massive echoing foyer. "If I had a house like this, after a hard day I'd probably disappear into my room and not come out again until I had to." She put her hands on her hips. "Wait. Aren't your parents teachers? How *do* you live in a place this nice?"

I rubbed my neck. "Ah, yeah, we inherited this house from my grandfather, Ignacio Ramírez."

"Wait . . . Your grandfather was Ignacio Ramírez, the trumpet player?" Her eyes bulged.

I sighed. "Does *everybody* know who my grandfather was?"

Andrea smirked. "Kind of hard not to. He was pretty famous—especially around here. I'm surprised his house wasn't on the Celebrity Homes of Miami tour."

"I guess you're right," I replied. "I know he was this big star. But it's weird. I haven't gotten used to it yet. This isn't how we lived in L.A., believe me." I tensed up as inspiration struck. "Anyway, it's hard to get comfortable in this house because it feels to me"—I checked to see if any of my family was still in earshot—"feels to me like it might be haunted!"

Andrea perked up. She slowly turned once again. "Oh

yes . . . I can tell your grandfather . . . left his mark on the place," she said, glancing up at the ginormous portrait of Abuelo, "but it's one of those classic old Coral Gables houses underneath. Probably has a million stories going back a hundred years. I can see that!"

Good, I thought. *If you can see that, maybe you'll be able to see Abuelo too!*

"Come on, let me give you the tour." Showing her around didn't make me feel less awkward about living in this giant mansion, but if I was going to learn from her how to handle a ghost, it needed to be done. I was curious to see what she would make of Abuelo when we ran into him.

Andrea had told me she could sense ghosts, and I guess she wasn't kidding, because she sensed them *everywhere*. In my bedroom, she said she felt the presence of a little girl. In the media room, it was two gangsters in suits. In the kitchen, an elderly lady stirring a pot of soup. Each time she would raise her voice and say things like *Hello? Can you communicate with us?* I wondered if she thought ghosts were hard of hearing.

"Wait," she said, at the entrance to the living room. "This is it! We're getting closer!"

Even though we'd struck out everywhere else in the house, my eyes widened just from her intensity. "What?"

She turned and whispered, "I think a murder may have been committed in this room!"

"A murder?" I knew Abuelo had a heart attack in this house, but that wasn't murder. In fact, he'd probably be insulted at the idea that anyone would want to kill the great Ignacio Ramírez.

She stalked across the room, past the alligator, toward the giant window. "Oh, definitely, and I think the ghost of the victim is stuck here . . . behind . . . this . . . curtain!"

She whooshed the curtain aside, and there *was* something there. I jumped backward in fright before realizing it was only Iggy.

Iggy gave us one half-curious look and lay back down on the floor.

I watched Andrea standing there, still holding the curtain back, her eyes narrowed as she peered around the room, looking for a spectral apparition.

I hadn't seen a little ghost girl, or two men in suits, or a murder victim. More important, I hadn't seen *Abuelo*. Where was he hiding, and why wasn't he showing himself?

"Why is your dog so skinny?" Andrea asked.

"He barely eats anything. Iggy was my grandfather's dog. I think he misses him, but if he doesn't start eating more soon, we're gonna have to take him to the vet, just in case."

Andrea petted Iggy's head and got the same half-hearted tail thump he gave everybody else.

Abuelo still wasn't showing himself, so I led Andrea to

the covered patio and got a couple of glasses of juice while she pulled out her script so we could continue reading where we left off.

"*All right, I'm here,*" she read. "*Don't lose your French fries. Why did you call me? What's wrong?*"

"Hang on," I said, running a finger down the page. "I can't find the line."

"*You've got to help me,*" she murmured.

"Oh, there it is! *Francine! You've got to help me!*"

"*What are you talking about? We already banished the evil fish stick to the dumpster dimension!*"

"*It's back! And now it's got company!*"

She held up a hand. "Hold on. I don't like how that sounds. Try 'and it brought some friends.'"

"*It's back! And it brought some friends!*"

"*Green beans, congealed gravy, rock-hard nuggets, spotty hamburger patty, mystery meat . . . thing. Jason, what's the connection?*"

"*Jason rubs his chin—*"

Andrea wadded up a bit of notebook paper and chucked it at me. "Don't read that part!"

"Oh! Right! Um, *It's all the foods nobody will eat.*"

Her eyes widened, and for a moment I thought she was reacting to something out on the patio with us. I turned to see if Abuelo had finally decided to join us.

"*Now they have a new life!*" she read. "*As monsters!*"

I turned hastily back to the table and scanned the script. *"These foods were already bad, but now they're EEEVIL!"*

She snorted at my overenunciation, and that started me giggling.

"Hang on a sec," she said, making some notes. "I'm really glad we're doing this. You hear a script differently when it's read aloud than when it's just words in your head. This is really helpful!"

I smiled, glad to be useful. Today's trumpet failure stung a little less while we were sitting here bringing Andrea's words to life.

We made it most of the way through act two before Andrea's phone buzzed and she read a text on the screen. "Ooh, my mom is here to pick me up," she said. "See you tomorrow?"

Something lurched in my gut at the thought of school the next day. I had managed to put this morning's band audition out of my mind for a little while, but soon enough I'd be right back in that room, right back on the spot, with the teacher and all the other kids watching me try to play trumpet. Which reminded me, I *really* needed to figure out where Abuelo had gone, if I had any chance of succeeding. The least he could do was show me where to find his trumpet. If I showed up to class needing to borrow one again, Mr. Edwards would send me right back to triangle city.

On the other hand, lunch today had been fun, and so

had running lines here at home. If I could just make it to lunch tomorrow, we'd do it all again. I could look forward to that, at least.

"Yeah," I replied as she gathered up the two copies of the script, her binder, and her pencils. "See you then!"

After I watched her leave, I turned back and caught sight of Abuelo leaning against the table. It was weird how I never saw him appear or disappear—instead, he always popped up wherever my attention wasn't focused.

"You see?" he said. "My lucky shirt worked! First day of school and already bringing a new friend home!"

I threw my hands in the air. "Why didn't you show yourself?"

His eyebrows shot up. "My boy! You had a pretty girl visiting you! I may have had many failings in life, but interfering between a boy and a cute girl was never one of them!"

My face heated up as I remembered that *look* Mami gave Papi and Cristina in the teacher parking lot. Did they all think Andrea was my new girlfriend or something? "She's my friend," I said. "And she can sense ghosts. She's, like, an expert in supernatural stuff. I wanted to find out if she could see you! If she can, maybe she can help us."

"Trust me, mi nieto! I was doing you a favor!"

I clenched my jaw. He wasn't listening. There seemed to be a lot of that going around. "Next time, don't hide! Show yourself!"

The patio door squeaked open, and I turned to see

Andrea peeking in. "Are you yelling at the dog? You shouldn't be so hard on him! It isn't easy when you lose somebody you love." She went silent after that, her eyes downcast.

"Andrea! You're back!"

She perked up. "Sorry, I forgot my backpack."

I glanced at Abuelo as she hurried to the table and grabbed the bag on the floor by her chair.

Abuelo shimmied over to where she stood. "Oooooh!" he said. "I am a ghooooost! Be very afraaaaaaid! Boooo!"

"Anyway," she said as she pulled all her stuff together, "I think you shouldn't stress so much about Iggy. He didn't only lose his master; he also has to get used to a whole new bunch of people he doesn't know. I bet he just needs time."

With that, she slung her bag over her shoulder, walked back to the patio door, passing right through Abuelo on her way, and left the two of us by ourselves.

I traded looks with the ghost of my grandfather.

"Some expert," he deadpanned.

My shoulders slumped. I guess I wasn't going to be getting advice on helping him cross over from Andrea the ghost hunter after all.

CHAPTER SIX

Abuelo paced the length of my room, walking right through all the junk we hadn't had a chance to move. Considering that all the stuff was *his,* and he was always showing up to "help" me, I was starting to feel like he was my roommate instead of my grandfather.

"Hola, hermosa," he said, gazing at his trumpet, which I'd brought to my room after dinner. It was beautiful. Thankfully, it hadn't been in any of the piles of boxes taking up space all over the house. His trumpet had a special place on a shelf in the media room. I hadn't noticed it because it was nestled lovingly in what Abuelo called a gig bag—soft brown leather on the outside, velvety black padding inside.

He had been proud to lead me to it after I explained what happened at school.

"It all makes sense now!" he said. "You are my grandson, my namesake—well, middle name, anyway—and now you're taking up my instrument. No wonder you are the only one who can see me! Clearly, we are meant to have a bond! Ay, mi nieto, I wish I'd had the opportunity to know you better before, in life."

I frowned. He was rich and traveled the world. Why *wouldn't* he have had the chance?

"You were actually in town the weekend of my fifth-grade graduation. I kept asking Papi if you would come, and Papi just told me that you were very busy."

"Oh, Benny, if I'd known about it, I would have come."

"Oh." I swallowed a lump in my throat. So Papi had never reached out to him.

Then I remembered how he and Papi didn't really talk, and how he and Abuela Gloria were divorced. That must have been why Papi never invited him to come spend time with us. They must not have gotten along.

"Mi nieto, that's all behind us. I'm here with you now, and the fact that you are joining the band is *fabulous*! There's no need for you to look so down!"

"Didn't you hear anything else I told you? I made a fool of myself today."

He harrumphed and shook his head. "That's part of the

artist's life, mi nieto. Do you have any idea how many times I've seen talented musicians make a fool of themselves?"

I propped myself up. "Including you?"

"Me?" Abuelo straightened. "Well, no, of course not *me*. But many other musicians! So many! Why, this one, uh, guitarist I knew, nobody came to his first show at all! And there was this, uh, other performer whose very first album review—" He paused midstride, leaned closer, and said, "Albums are what we used to call—"

"I know what albums are, Abuelo."

"Well, it was a one-sentence review: 'A gimmicky impersonation of the classic acts of Cuba's golden big-band era.'" He put his hands on his hips. "¿Qué clase de estupidez es *gimmicky*? Are horns a gimmick now?"

"I thought you said this was a guitar—"

"Yes, guitars, horns, pianos, it was a whole band, and you are missing the point!"

"Sorry," I whispered. He sure was upset about a review some other musician got.

He bent over until his face was inches from mine, and I realized I could see the shelf on the far side of the room clearly through his forehead.

"Do you want to be great?"

I blinked. "Uh—yes?"

"Then you need to get comfortable being laughed at by people who are less talented than you, until one day they realize how talented you are, and *then* they stop laughing."

"That's . . ." I swallowed. "That's terrific, Abuelo. Really great advice. There's just one little problem . . . almost nothing, really, just a little thing. I think you may have forgotten that *I actually cannot play the trumpet*!"

He turned away and resumed his pacing. "Nonsense! The talent is in you! It is genetic! You just have to act like it." He tried to pick up a trophy, swiped his hand through it with no effect, and brushed his hair back instead. "Half of being a great musician is showmanship, presentation, and attitude!"

"Abuelo, that's three things—"

"Hush! Are you ready for me to show you how to become great?"

I straightened at that. Finally—less talk and more teaching! "Yes! I'm ready!" I jumped off the bed, opened the trumpet case, and took out his old horn.

"Put that away, mi nieto!"

"Huh?"

He stood with his hands spread out, like he was welcoming an audience to his concert. "That instrument has played in concert halls that are more than a century old. It has played at the weddings of dignitaries. It has played in front of royalty. If you want it to make music for you, you must treat it with the love and respect it deserves. You don't play a horn like this in blue jeans and a mustard-stained T-shirt. You need to look the part. The first thing we need to work on is your look. Go find my scrapbook and that bag of clothes you rescued from your mother!"

ON THE RIDE to school the next day, Papi glanced at me in the rearview mirror at least once per block. Beside me, Manny kept leaning over and murmuring to Cristina, and they would both giggle like hyenas at the zoo.

I stared out the window. If I pretended not to notice, I wouldn't have to try to justify the fashion choices I'd made—the fashion choices Abuelo had made for me.

He had picked out a purple shirt with silver sequins around the cuffs and collar. The shirt was big on me, but I paired it with the itchy black dress pants from the suit my parents bought me so I could attend one of Papi's TV show premieres. With Abuelo barking orders and trying to guide my hands, I had combed my hair upward from my face and shaped it into a shellacked mountain with extra-hold styling gel. I was a living re-creation of Ignacio in one of the scrapbook photos.

It had worked for him; it would work for me too. Abuelo said this was how to be a star musician, and if anybody would know, it would be him.

Next to me, Manny and Cristina snorted and giggled again.

"Laugh it up," I said. "We'll see who's laughing when I'm a success."

Manny quirked an eyebrow. "What are you gonna succeed in? Dressing like an alien? Are you gonna be in a fashion show on Mars?"

Cristina grinned. "Your hair is taller than a skyscraper!"

Manny laughed so hard he collapsed onto me. It was all I could do not to shove him back onto Cristina's side. "You look like you're in Aladdin cosplay—as the Cave of Wonders!"

Cristina chortled. To be fair, it *was* actually kind of funny.

All they could see was the clothes. They didn't know Abuelo was coaching me. Last night he had worked with me on my stance until I was ready to pass out. Even now I could hear his barked orders of *Feet shoulder-width apart! Chest out! Bend your knees a little! Lean back!*

He'd even shown me how to hold the trumpet. He said the rest was instinct, and it would kick in when I committed to acting the part. Was that so different from what Manny and Cristina did?

I leaned forward to make eye contact with Cristina. "Hey, I don't make fun of your frilly tutus and your sweaty ballet slippers." Nudging Manny, I added, "And I didn't say anything about it when you were going around dressed like the sun."

Cristina leaned away. "But those are related to the arts that we practice all the time. What does dressing like a giant diamond-studded grape have to do with playing the trumpet?"

Mami turned around in the front seat. "Manny, Cristina, leave him alone. I've always said that I want you kids to be brave enough to be yourselves and not worry about what other people think." Elbowing Papi, she added, "¿De acuerdo?"

"Eh? Uh, yeah. Sure. I want you to be yourself." He met my eyes in the mirror. "If that's what this is."

I swallowed. Papi of all people would recognize his father's style.

Under his breath, Manny murmured, "I'll give you one thing, bro. You *look* like jazz *sounds*."

Cristina giggled, but I wasn't sure if Manny was still making fun of me or if he was seeing my point. That was . . . *almost* not an insult.

None of which changed the fact that once we parked, I had to walk through school. Having your sister and brother laugh at you was one thing—but total strangers was another.

"Wait, is there a costume contest today?" one kid said as he passed me, eyeing my shirt.

"If there is, dude, he wins. That's the best Ignacio Ramírez costume I've ever *seen*."

I did my best to ignore the sound of them high-fiving each other and snickering as they continued down the hall. All I had wanted was to fit in at this school, and now I was purposely doing the opposite. But when your grandfather gives you advice, you take it. When an internationally renowned star musician gives you advice, you take it. When a ghost gives you advice, you take it. And when those three are the same person, well then, you'd *really* better take it.

As I carried Abuelo's trumpet case through the halls on my way to first period, I did my best to take deep breaths and keep my mouth from drying up. Over and over again, I repeated Abuelo's reminders in my head: *You're a natural. Head high, chest out. Act like a star and it's only a matter of time until the world figures out you are one.*

I headed to class early, because the last thing I wanted to do was linger in the hallway. Mr. Edwards let me in as soon as he saw me through the window, his forehead wrinkling as he took in my outfit.

"Well," he said, taking a seat on his stool. "You certainly look . . . festive." He picked up a pencil like he was going to write something down in his notebook, but he just tapped it absently against the metal music stand in front of him.

"Er, thanks," I said, scratching at the left knee of my slacks.

"Why don't we go ahead and see how it sounds now, before everybody else gets here?"

He meant before I humiliated myself, I figured, but honestly, I was fine with that. I opened the trumpet case, picked up the horn, and took a deep breath. I put it to my lips the way Abuelo showed me, closed my eyes, and willed the Ramírez family talent to pour into me.

And when I could stall no more, I blew.

Mr. Edwards stopped me after about an hour, or maybe it was fifteen seconds. The room was still empty, so I guess it couldn't have been too long.

"Hey . . . ah . . . well . . ." He chewed on his lip, and I felt myself slump. "You're holding the trumpet right this time, so that's good. Maybe it's starting to come back to you a little?"

My face heated up. "Maybe."

Mr. Edwards leaned forward. "You know what I think might be holding you back, kiddo?" Without waiting for an answer, he leapt to his feet and went to his desk, which was in the back corner of the room. He grabbed his phone and tapped on the screen for a few seconds. Just when I was starting to wonder if he'd forgotten that I was there, he held it out to me. "Check out this picture. I took it nine years ago, at the stage door behind the Jackie Gleason Theater, after a concert."

I stared at a blurry photo. It was dark, and mostly I saw the backs of a bunch of people's heads. Some of them were holding up CDs or books. Separated from the crowd by a barrier was a tan man in a gray guayabera with a giant red setting sun splashed across the front, with "gems" at the ends of each ray, and—

"It's Abu— It's my grandfather!" I stared up at Mr. Edwards. "You saw him in concert?"

He nodded and grinned. "Oh yeah! He was terrific! It

was at least a decade since 'Miami Maravilloso' had come out, but he still had it. That double high C? Amazing! And he held it for so long! And his stage presence . . . What a huge personality!" He paused. "But here's the thing. You know who he looks like?"

"Who?"

Mr. Edwards held the phone up beside me. "You. Or you look like him." He frowned. "I can't tell what's going on just yet: whether you're a trumpet player who's a little . . . well, a *lot* rusty, or what. But it seems to me like you're trying really hard to fill your grandfather's shoes. And, uh, his stage clothes too. I can't figure out if that means you need to find your own style, or if it means you only want to be a trumpet player because it's what you think your grandfather would want."

Was that a question? I took a breath to answer, but I had no idea what to say, so I was almost grateful when he answered for me.

"My two cents? You're getting in your own way. Here's what I think will help, kiddo. Tomorrow, why don't you come to school as Benny Ramírez—but keep using *your* trumpet, because clearly, you're better off with that one than with a loaner. Who knows? Maybe you just need a couple of days to shake the rust off. Or if not, it's early enough in the year that we can find another arts placement. It doesn't have to be this."

He smiled, his eyebrows up in that friendly way teachers do when they are acting like they are your buddy instead of the person with the power to redirect your whole life. He thought he was being nice, but his message was clear—figure it out, or get kicked out of the band.

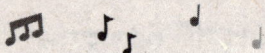

GOING TO a school full of creative, artistic students had its downsides—like when they decided to mock you, they knew how to *really* mock you. At lunch, somebody had apparently nicknamed me Eggplantio Ramírez, and for the rest of my classes all I heard were whispers—*stage* whispers, of course—of the name.

It was so bad that when I saw Cristina in the parking lot after school and took one look at her—sagging on a bench and staring at her feet—I thought at first that she'd heard about my day and was embarrassed for me.

"It's not as bad as it sounds," I said. "I'll be okay."

She did this weird kind of double take. "Huh?"

I held up my arms and gave my best jazz hands. "You know, Eggplantio Ramírez?" I let my gaze wander. "You're worried that people will make fun of you because you're my sister, right?"

She turned halfway toward me. "I have no idea what you're talking about."

"Then why do you look like you just lost a footrace to a mannequin?"

After a moment, she sighed and said, "I didn't get the part, Benny."

I didn't say anything right away, because those words coming from Cristina's lips just didn't make sense.

"Who did?"

"Sarah," she said. The same girl she had been talking about yesterday. The one who was mean and full of herself.

"Oh no." The seconds dragged on. Here is where a better brother would have come up with something supportive to say. Finally, I settled for "What part did you get?"

Cristina stared into the distance. "I don't know. Ms. Cassidy hasn't announced all the parts yet. She said she'd let us know by Thursday. But she flat-out said that Sarah would be the Sugarplum Fairy."

It didn't make sense. Actually, I *could* think of one explanation. "I bet the teacher just gave it to her because she already knows her, or because she doesn't want the other kids to think you're getting special treatment because of our parents."

Cristina sniffed but said nothing.

"Is this girl any good?"

It took her a few seconds to answer. "Yeah. She's good."

I caught the words *Is she as good as you?* just microseconds before they came out of my mouth. Hey, I was getting better at this.

"I bet she's not as good as you are."

"Thanks." Cristina shrugged. "I probably got Dewdrop," she went on. "It's a good . . . well . . ." She sniffed. "It's not a bad part. I've just never had to . . ."

I knew what she meant. She didn't have to finish that sentence because we both knew how it ended. She'd never had to play second fiddle.

For me, second fiddle would be an upgrade. But unlike her, I hadn't come into the school as some kind of prodigy. I'd *expected* to fall flat on my face, and I *did,* and now the whole school was talking about the Great Eggplantio.

Our brother showed up while we were each lost in our own moping.

"Hey, Manny," I said, hoping he would notice Cristina's mood and hold off on talking about his latest acting success.

He'd been walking with his hands in his pockets and his head down, but at my words he turned his gaze on me slowly and gave me a weird fake grin.

"Oh, yeah, sorry," I said. "Hi, Seymour."

"I'm not Seymour," he said, his voice drawn out and hitting a couple of the words in falsetto. "I'm Cheshy. The cat."

I blinked. "You mean the one from *Alice in Wonderland*?"

He bowed his head and gestured as though he were tipping a hat. "The very saaaaame."

"Is that the part you got?"

"Indeeeed," he said, somehow stretching it out to three syllables.

"Congrats," mumbled Cristina. "At least one of us isn't a loser."

From the sidewalk outside the fenced-in lot, a boy I didn't know called out, "Hey, new kid!"

That could have meant any of us, but Manny looked up and nodded in recognition. He approached the fence. "Not to be parliamentaaaaarian, but we're allll new kidsss, to an octogenarian," he said, oddly overenunciating half his words.

Manny's classmate turned to his friends, who both shrugged. "Um, okay. Anyway, congratulations on the part. That's really good for your first audition here. I'm Angel—you're Manny, right?"

"In the flesh-y, but I anssssswer to Cheshy."

"Huh? But this morning, you said—"

"I knowwwwww who I was this morrrrning, but I have chaaaaanged a few times since then."

Angel blinked. "Ohhh, I get it. You're staying in character. Uh, cool. Anyway . . . see you around, new kid." Before Manny could answer, the group hurried away, snickering quietly among themselves.

"He's so weird," I heard one of them say.

I turned to Manny. "Um, looks like you're getting to know your castmates."

He grinned at me, a creepy smile that showed all his

teeth—and I mean, literally all his teeth. Gradually the smile left his eyes, but not his mouth. The effect was unsettling. When he finally closed his lips, I sighed with relief. "We're all maaaaad here," he finally said.

I took a seat on the back bumper of our SUV. I didn't really know what to say, and anyway, I didn't want to talk with Cheshy *or* Seymour; I wanted to talk with Manny.

Finally, our parents showed up, and it felt like I could put the day behind me. Except I couldn't, because they kept asking questions about how our day had gone. Just like yesterday, Cristina and I pretty much kept to yes or no answers. Manny . . . well, I guess Manny gave catlike answers, but since nobody could tell what he was talking about, he might as well have kept quiet.

"Congratulations on getting the Cheshire Cat, Manny," Papi said. "I heard some of the drama kids were having a pizza party this weekend. I'm surprised you haven't said anything about it."

Manny perked up for just a second, and then deflated like an old balloon. In that moment, it felt like a flash went off in my head. He didn't say anything about the party because he didn't know. Nobody invited him.

For an instant, Manny was sitting next to me, and then something in his posture changed and he was the cat again. "Dairy gives catsss diarrhea. And anyway, felinesssss arenn't allowed in pizzerias."

I rubbed the back of my neck. I thought at least Manny

was getting what he wanted out of this school because he got a good part in the play. But he was getting the cold shoulder from all the other kids.

It was official. All three of the Ramírez kids had struck out today.

CHAPTER SEVEN

Mr. Edwards was absent the next morning, so after three days I *still* wasn't kicked out of band. It was probably too much to hope that I might one-day-at-a-time my way into staying, but I'd worry about that another day.

When Andrea asked if I wanted to come over after school, I said yes—and *then* remembered to ask my parents.

"I don't know," Mami said. After lunch, I'd gone out of my way to stop by her classroom because I'd figured she'd be more likely than Papi to say yes. Students were just beginning to file in and take their seats, and Mami's whiteboard was already full of verb conjugations in her neat red handwriting. Next to *bailo, bailas, baila, bailamos, bailan,* she'd drawn a couple of stick figures dancing. "We haven't finished unpacking, and your grandmother is coming down from Tampa for the weekend. Since Gloria will be here soon, I want the house to be presentable."

"Please?" I asked, trying to keep it down so all her students wouldn't witness me begging my mom for stuff. "Abuela won't expect the place to be perfect—the whole reason she's coming is to help!"

"There's imperfect and there's a wreck. Someday maybe you'll have in-laws, and then you'll understand."

"We still have until Saturday morning before she gets here." And then I played my best card: "You want us to make friends in our new school, right?"

She gave me a thoughtful look. "You said Andrea's house? That's the girl who visited us, right?" She got that same expression on her face that she'd had when she was communicating telepathically with Papi and Cristina. "I suppose we can spare you for a few hours."

I hadn't gotten kicked out of band *and* I had gotten permission to hang out with Andrea. *Must be my lucky day,* I thought.

Andrea couldn't see my ghost, but maybe I'd be able to see hers. Was it weird that I wasn't scared? Then again, Abuelo wasn't scary. Maybe ghosts were like living people—some were mean, but just as many, or more, were nice.

I met Andrea by the back parking lot after school, but instead of heading to the cars, she led me to the gate.

"Where's your mom?" I asked.

"Kitchen staff stays later than students, taking everything apart and cleaning it and prepping for breakfast. I usually walk home, unless it's pouring."

"Oh. Um, makes sense."

Andrea had chains that dangled from belt loop to belt loop on her black jeans, and as she walked, they jingled in time to her footsteps, like car keys or loose change. I kept catching myself unintentionally walking at her pace, as though she were a percussionist in a marching band.

For the first few blocks, we wandered past single-story homes on huge tree-filled plots of land. Gradually, though, the houses grew taller and closer together as we passed apartment complexes and office buildings. The smell of cut grass got replaced with exhaust fumes, and the chirping of birds got drowned out by car engines and horns.

As we walked, Andrea talked about school and people I didn't know and where she had gone before. I did my best to listen, but I probably missed some things.

"Look out!" she said at one corner, grabbing my arm and tugging me back. She had kept me from tripping right off the curb. "Haven't you been in a city before?"

"I come from L.A.," I said.

"Then why are you gawking like a tourist, staring up at every building instead of paying attention to where you're walking?"

I thought for a moment, and then realized why. "We got into town the day before school started. We've been so busy getting settled in, this is basically the first chance I've had to see anything."

She stopped abruptly. "Oh, you're not seeing anything yet. This is the most *ordinary* part of Miami. Strip malls and office buildings. Someday on a weekend you should come over and I can get my mom to take us sightseeing. There are all kinds of artsy shops and parks right on the water here in Coconut Grove and even a place that makes nothing but milkshakes. Or we can go to Calle Ocho and Little Havana. We could play dominoes on one of the permanent tables they have, and get the best Cuban food, and on Fridays they have music and dancing. Even South Beach would be more interesting than *this*."

I blinked. "Oh. That sounds cool."

She nodded. "It is," she agreed, and started walking again.

We reached a giant palm-lined street, and I was worried we'd need to find a way across, but Andrea turned us to the right.

Taking in the signs, the buildings, and most of all, the elevated railway that ran alongside the highway, I said, "I think we were on this street the day we moved in!"

"Yeah," she said. "I'd be surprised if you weren't. This is US 1. It's basically the biggest street in Miami." Turning up a driveway to a small peach-colored apartment building with an orange clay tile roof, she added, "It's also home. We're here."

I climbed a set of narrow stone stairs to the second floor

and watched while she pulled a key out from a chain around her neck and let us in.

Her apartment probably could have fit in Abuelo's living room and still left space for the alligator. But while Abuelo's house felt like a museum to his career, this apartment actually seemed designed to be comfortable. I saw bookshelves on either side of the TV, so overfilled that books were stacked on their sides to use up all the available space. On the wall over the couch were plastic-framed movie posters from old black-and-white horror and science fiction movies. Under the TV was a video game controller, and on the shelf in front of it were . . . plastic bugs?

I wanted to browse her bookshelves for anything familiar. I wanted to ask about the bugs. I wanted to check out her video games. All that seemed nosy, though, so I glanced through her window at the view. Seeing a 7-Eleven on the street below, I said, "Oh, cool! If I lived here, I'd want a Slurpee every single day!"

"Yeah. Too bad they're not free."

"True. Um, we should get to work."

She spread her notebooks out on the coffee table. "Okay, top of act three. Francine and Jason are barricaded in the cafeteria bathroom."

"Which one?"

She frowned. "Which what?"

"Which bathroom? Boys'? Girls'? One of the faculty ones?"

"Does it matter?"

"Well, I don't think Jason would want to go in the girls' room."

"He would if he were being chased by possessed cafeteria food!"

True. "Fine. *Help me hold the door, Francine! The avalanche of food is pushing me back!*" I rubbed my chin. "How are you going to stage this? Are you going to use actual food?"

"Of course. Why wouldn't I?" Andrea replied.

"Because it would be really messy and gross."

"That's why it would be awesome!" she said, nodding. "Anyway, stop interrupting." She focused on her pages. *"There. I got the door locked."*

"How would Francine be able to do that?"

She cocked her head. "By flipping the latch."

I shook my head. "The bathroom doors are keyed on both sides. Only a custodian would be able to lock it."

"How do you even know that? You've only been at this school for two days."

I shrugged. "When you keep mistaking that bathroom for history class, you notice these things."

"Look," she said, "I'll put in a note to add a moment where Francine grabs a set of keys dropped by a fleeing custodian. Happy? Now read your line!"

"Look out! Haunted tartar sauce is oozing in under the door!"

We lost another fifteen minutes arguing about how long

it would take for enough tartar sauce to ooze in for it to be a drowning hazard, and whether or not Jason or Francine would really describe the sauce as *ectoplasmic boogers*.

I kept wanting to tell her about Abuelo, but I couldn't figure out how to do it. Which sounds silly—I mean, it wasn't like I didn't know how to open my mouth and make words come out. But I hadn't told anybody else yet, not even my family. To be fair, none of them would have believed me anyway. Andrea at least believed in ghosts. But I kept waiting for her to say something kind of related, so I could say *Speaking of dead people who live in our houses . . . Have I got a story for you!*

While we were working, her mom came home, kissed Andrea, and said hi to me. I'd only seen her mom from a distance—even last night at our house, Andrea had gone out while I stayed behind on the patio with Abuelo. Up close, I saw that Ms. Wade had the build and posture of an army sergeant, which made her soft voice and easy smile surprising.

"I stopped by the grocery store on the way home for something to cook for dinner," she announced. "Benny, are you allergic to anything?"

After I assured her that I had no allergies or dietary restrictions, she disappeared into the kitchen to prepare dinner. At Abuelo's house, we hadn't gotten moved in enough to start making meals at home—it was still takeout every night.

It wasn't long before Andrea's apartment filled with the

aroma of pork, beans, scallions, and rice. It was hard to believe this delicious perfume was coming from the same person who cooked the slop we were getting at school. I started finding it hard to concentrate on Andrea's play.

"Dinner's almost ready," Andrea's mom finally called out. "Andie, can you set the table, please?"

"Andie?" I asked as we got up from the couch.

She pointed a finger at me. "Do not."

I held my hands up in surrender. "Okay! I heard nothing!"

I followed her into the eat-in kitchen and carried plates and silverware to the table.

Ms. Wade stood at the stove, and I saw that in addition to pork, she had prepared green beans, which I would have to pretend to like, and rice and black beans, which I would not.

"Everything looks great," I said. Andrea rolled her eyes like she thought I was kissing up to her mom.

"Thanks, Benny. The only thing I'm disappointed in is the black beans. In a perfect world, I would have prepared them from scratch, but that would take hours, so I settled for canned. I added some onion flakes, cumin, and some garlic to give it flavor, but it's just . . . off."

We usually used canned beans too, but when Abuela came over, she would spend an entire weekend preparing them—rinsing hard, dry beans from a bag, and then letting them soak in cold water overnight. In the morning she would make a sofrito—basically an herb-filled sauce where most of the flavor came from. The house would smell like onions, garlic, sweet peppers, and cilantro, making my mouth water and my stomach rumble as they simmered all day long. I couldn't blame Ms. Wade for just heating up some beans from a can.

Andrea dipped a spoon in the beans and tasted them. "Needs more salt."

Her mom sighed. "You always want to dump salt on everything."

"That's 'cause salt makes things taste good!"

Her mother shook her head. "You're hopeless." She peered at me thoughtfully for a moment, picked up another spoon, and said, "Benny, do you want to taste it and tell me what you think?"

"Sure!" I said.

I tasted the beans, and I could see what she meant. I could taste the spices she added, but something was still off. I thought about the flavors I associated with my abuela's arroz con frijoles.

"They're not bad, but if you added just a little bit of vinegar, I bet that would really make it pop."

"Oh, that sounds like a good idea." Ms. Wade rooted around in a cupboard and pulled out a pair of small bottles. "White or red?"

What would Abuela do? "Red. Definitely red."

She gave the bottle a brief shake over the pot and stirred

the mix. After letting the beans simmer for a few more minutes, she tasted them again.

"Oh! This is so much better! My goodness, Benny, you were absolutely right! How did you know?"

I dug my hands in my pockets. "Umm . . . I just suggested stuff my family uses when they cook."

"Maybe," she said, "but you could tell from tasting the beans what wasn't already there. That means you have a sophisticated palate, and good instincts! That's real talent!"

My face heated up. It's not like I never got praised for the things I did, but nobody ever told me I was *talented* at something. Not like Cristina or Manny. I thought about how Andrea said they used to have a home economics class with a big focus on cooking at the school but now they didn't. That was too bad, because at least in a cooking class I wouldn't have to worry about bursting people's eardrums while making a pot of rice.

After we finished eating and cleared the table, Andrea asked, "You wanna see the rest of the apartment? I mean, it's no mansion, but . . ."

"Definitely!"

I followed her down a hallway that led away from the living room. On the right side of the hallway was a narrow little table, cluttered with a mirror, a couple of framed photos, a set of keys, and other knickknacks. As she passed by, Andrea absentmindedly dug into her pocket and pulled out some crushed white flowers with bursts of yellow in the centers and dropped them into a decorative bowl.

"What are those?" I asked.

She startled a bit, as if she hadn't even noticed what she was doing. "Oh. These are bulltongues. They grow wild by the canal we passed on our way here, and I grab some when I walk past in the morning. It's to let any spirits know that I welcome them and mean them no harm. You're actually supposed to use daisies, but these are what I can find, and they look kind of like daisies."

I struggled to imagine this girl in her black jeans and her scary T-shirt and dangling chains stopping to pick flowers by the side of the canal.

Leaning closer, I asked, "Do you actually know that you have ghosts here?"

"Any building that has been around for a long time has them," she said, walking again. "This building has been here for, like, seventy years." She pointed at a clock hanging on the wall between two bedroom doors. "This clock is always seven minutes fast. We fix it all the time, but it just gets ahead again."

I checked the time on my phone. She was right, seven minutes. "The clock in my parents' SUV is the same way," I said. "They like it that way, though, because it helps them keep from running late."

"That's the thing," Andrea replied. "Last summer I tried not fixing it, to see if it would keep gaining time, maybe get ten or fifteen or thirty minutes fast, and it didn't. It just stayed seven minutes ahead."

"Huh. Weird. But, um, what does that have to do with ghosts?"

"Ghosts are known to use technology as a way to reach from their dimension into ours. Glitches are one of the most common signs of ghosts."

I tilted my head. "Is a clock *technology*?"

She put her hands on her hips. "Do *you* know how to make one? Technology doesn't have to mean computers. Besides, ghosts also like to move stuff, so moving the minute hand counts."

"Okay," I said with a shrug.

Andrea narrowed her eyes at me. "Not convinced? Fine. Wait till you see what's in my room!" She stomped off, and I followed her through a door covered in black construction-paper bats.

I'd expected Andrea's bedroom to be something like Cristina's—not dance-focused, of course, but pink, with model horses or something, maybe an old dollhouse from when she was a little kid. Once I saw her actual room, though—with two bookshelves surrounding her bed and posters for old horror movies on the wall—I realized that made no sense. This was *Andrea*.

"See this crack?" she asked, pointing to the window behind her desk.

"Uh-huh."

"It just happened one day last February. I was sitting right there writing a comic book, so I can tell you, nothing hit it, nobody did anything. One moment the window was fine, and a second later it was cracked."

"Oh. Um, spooky."

"Right? Also, get up close and look down at that tree's roots."

The view out her window was of the building's parking lot, but there was maybe fifteen feet of grass between the building and the asphalt, and in that space was a massive old oak tree with a gnarled root system. "What about them?"

She traced a pattern on the windowpane—not the cracked one—and I did my best to follow along. "See?" she asked. "Letters." Running her finger on the glass, she spelled out, "A-N-E-A."

I kind of saw it. "Anea? Is that a name?"

She turned to me. "Don't you get it? It's trying to spell ANDREA. It's . . . my grandmother. She used to take care of me, since my mom was working all the time, and then she . . ." Andrea swallowed. "She isn't with us anymore. I think she misses me."

I chewed on my lip. That tree had to be decades old, and if Andrea's grandmother took care of her, then obviously decades hadn't passed since her death. I was starting to think Andrea hadn't actually seen any ghosts at all.

Maybe her grandmother's ghost was out there and missing her granddaughter. But more likely, it was Andrea who missed her grandmother.

Then again, anybody else would think *I* was imagining *my* ghost grandparent, so maybe I was nobody to judge here.

"I bet she does miss you," I finally said, carefully tracing the crack on her windowpane.

I really wished she had been able to see Abuelo when she came over. It would have been nice not having to keep this secret all to myself. But of all the people I'd met since moving here, Andrea was the only one who would have understood. The only one who would have listened.

She still could, I suppose.

I hesitated for a moment, and then decided to dive in. "I have a ghost too. My grandfather."

I felt nervous waiting for her reaction, but lighter, like the secret I'd been keeping was a giant rock I'd been carrying, and now I'd finally put it down.

She blinked. "No you don't. I was in your house. Your grandfather's not there. I would have sensed it."

For a moment, I felt heat rise from my gut to my head. Here I was saying I believed her when all she had was stuff like a fast clock and some random tree roots, and she just stood there and flat out *told* me I was wrong about Abuelo?

"Are you—" I cut myself off and took a deep breath. "I believe you," I said. I didn't like how whiny I sounded, but whiny was probably better than telling her off. "Why can't you believe me?"

Andrea sat on her bed. "You probably just think your grandfather is haunting you because your house is filled with ghosts. Common rookie mistake."

"No . . . I think my grandfather is haunting me because . . . he's haunting me! He showed up in my bedroom to give me fashion advice and music lessons."

Her eyes narrowed. "You're making fun of me!"

"I promise I'm not."

She peered at me, like she was trying to look into my brain and see if I was lying. For a moment, I worried she would ask me for proof. If there was one person I thought might have believed me, it would have been her, but now I wasn't so sure saying anything had been a good idea.

She let out a breath. "Well, maybe he's only revealing his presence to people he has some connection to, and that's why I couldn't sense him." She leaned forward. "What does he talk about?"

I sat on her desk chair. "He thinks I need help to not be a loser. So he's been trying to teach me to be a musician, like him. He's showing me how to play the trumpet."

She cocked her head. "Like, scales and stuff?"

"Um, not so much that. He's, uh, taught me the best hair gel to use to get maximum height. How to walk into a room like you own it. Star stuff." At the expression on her face, I quickly added, "I'm sure we'll get to music too, though."

She nodded. "I guess that makes sense. He would want somebody to carry on his legacy, and you said neither your brother nor your sister is a musician."

"I don't think it's about his legacy. He says he went to the, uh, tunnel or the light or whatever it is people see when they die, and they told him he had unfinished business, and if he wanted to move on, he had to take care of it by New Year's."

"That's awfully specific." She frowned. "His unfinished business is for you to play the trumpet? How does that make sense? That would be *your* business, not his."

I stared at the carpet on her floor, mentally tracing the pile. "I may have told him I wasn't good at anything. And, uh, I almost never saw my grandfather when he was alive. I think maybe he believes that if he succeeds in helping me be a star, he'll earn his wings."

She crossed her legs. "I've read a lot about ghosts—in addition to my own experiences, of course. And I've just never heard of anything like that. . . . Ghosts sometimes stick around to haunt somebody who has wronged them, or they stick around because *they* wronged somebody else, and they need to make amends."

I stiffened, feeling an inexplicable need to defend Abuelo. "Well, Ignacio Ramírez never wronged anybody. He was the greatest, and everybody loved him, so that's a dead end. Unless we come up with something that makes more sense, I'm going to focus on making this band thing work."

MAMI PICKED ME UP a little after eight. She was quiet on the way home, not singing along to oldies on the radio like she usually did when she drove. She just gripped the wheel tightly and glanced at the clock on the center console about once per block. I had a feeling she was thinking about Abuela's upcoming visit and how we were running out of time to get the house in order before she arrived. Though they got along well, Mami always stressed out before Abuela's visits.

I was stressed too. I'd dodged a bullet with the postponed band audition today, and I'd done all I could to put it out of my mind while I was with Andrea. But as I stared out the window at the massive trees and the spooky shadows they cast from the coppery streetlights, I realized the audition was more of a boomerang than a bullet, because it was coming around again tomorrow.

"You know," I said, leaning forward in the backseat, "we should play hooky tomorrow. We can get the house ready, and then maybe go see a movie!"

She shook her head with a smile. "Nice try, Benny. But if I have to go to school tomorrow, so do you."

I slumped back in my seat with a sigh. Oh well. It was worth a shot.

When we got home, I saw that hardly a dent had been made in all the mess. But I couldn't say anything, since I hadn't been there to pitch in. Cristina kept walking around like a zombie, instead of her usual shtick of pirouetting everywhere she went. Manny was still doing his Cheshy routine, except he kept trailing off and falling out of character. I couldn't make up my mind whether that was a bad thing or a good one.

"Finally! You're back!"

I managed not to jump when Abuelo appeared in the kitchen.

"I've seen wakes livelier than this place!" he said. "What is up with everybody?"

He followed me into the living room, but I knew better than to try to answer him in front of my family. Instead, I looked at some of the stuff we needed to move. I hadn't helped all day, but maybe if I cleared away some of this junk, everybody else would be able to relax a bit.

Someone had filled some boxes, though there was plenty that wouldn't fit inside a box, like that cutout of Abuelo pitching High Peak Water. I picked up one that was labeled STUFF.

Manny had to have written that one. Only he or I would have labeled anything STUFF. I grabbed it by the openings and tugged. It was heavy, but not too much for me to lift.

"Where are we putting . . . *stuff*?" I asked nobody in particular.

"That 'stuff' came from fans who loved my music," Abuelo said glumly.

"Put it in the garage," Papi called from the master suite.

Abuelo kept me company as I lugged the carton to the garage. "There's a folder in there filled with thank-you notes from kids at a summer camp for aspiring musicians. Several of them colored drawings of me."

I wondered if he could see through cardboard. Who knew what was possible for a ghost?

"There's also a mosaic of the Miami skyline made entirely from fingernail clippings." He grimaced. "That one I don't love as much. Clearly, somebody put a lot of time into making it for me, though."

I gagged at the thought of having art made of somebody else's fingernails. And then I gagged again when I realized that now I *did* have exactly that.

The thought of what was inside seemed to make the box weigh more. I huffed at the strain. Since he wouldn't help me carry anything, I considered asking Abuelo to leave me alone until it was time to plan for tomorrow. I knew I was being unfair, though. I was sure he would have helped me if he could have. Probably.

Back in the living room, I examined another box. CONCERT PROGRAMS, it said, in Cristina's pretty flowing letters.

"Where do you want the concert programs?" I called out.

"Where do we want what?" Papi yelled back.

"Abuelo's concert programs."

"Garage!"

Again with the garage. At least the programs would be lighter.

Except they weren't. Maybe Cristina had labeled them wrong? I felt more like I was carrying bowling balls, or maybe bricks. I tried to drag the box off the top of its stack, and accidentally sent it tumbling to the ground, popping the lid off and spilling its contents. It actually *was* filled with programs. I picked one up. Apparently, each program was pretty light, but put several hundred of them in one container, and it might as well be filled with lead.

"Careful, mi nieto."

"*Now* you tell me," I said, rolling my eyes. Raising my voice, I called out, "Can someone help me carry this?"

Papi stuck his head out. "Benny, your mom and I are busy trying to make room for our own stuff. Why don't you just leave anything that's too heavy for later?"

"Be a lot easier if you just left my stuff alone," Abuelo grumbled.

I looked at the pile. Honestly, *everything* seemed too heavy. "Why don't I work on bringing the trophies from my bedroom to the downstairs room. It'll be lighter, and at least I know where you want them."

"You are taking my trophies *where*?"

Papi rubbed his chin. "Actually, the trophies aren't really

in anybody's way right now. There's a lot of things you could do besides unpacking that will help make this house presentable for when your grandmother gets here. I'll make you a list."

"The trophies are in *my* way," I said under my breath. At the same time, Abuelo straightened and asked, "¿Qué? When *who* gets here?"

Papi heard neither of us, though. He disappeared into the master suite and came out a minute later with a used envelope on the back of which he had written enough chores to keep me busy for the rest of the school year.

Taking out the garbage was probably the easiest task, so I headed to the kitchen to empty the fancy trash compactor.

"What is Félix talking about?" Abuelo asked, following me from room to room. "Which grandmother? Gloria? *My* Gloria?"

I *mm-hmm*ed an answer, hoping that if anybody overheard me, they would think nothing of it. It was all I could do not to remind him that he was divorced, so no, not *his* Gloria.

"She is coming here?" he went on. "Why is she coming here? This is *my* house!"

Looking around first to make sure nobody was watching, I murmured, "I guess she's coming to visit *us,* because we're her family."

"But . . . but . . . that woman almost ruined my life!"

CHAPTER EIGHT

"What?" I stared at him. Abuela? A life-ruiner? Doubtful.

"I can't believe she's coming to *my* house, mi nieto! Why would she even want to do that? Who would want to go to their dead ex's home?"

"She's coming to help us," I grunted, lugging the heavy bag of garbage out the side door to the garage and putting it in the can.

"I just feel like your parents should have given this more thought."

"Uh-huh." I dragged the can out to the curb. What should they have thought of? The feelings of a ghost they didn't even know about?

"And anyway, what could she do to help? There are five of you, all young and in your prime!"

"I guess." I held up Papi's list so I could read it in the distant light coming from beside the front door. Next up was the pool.

"She's always hated everything having to do with my career—all she's going to want to do is throw everything out!"

I led the way around the plant-filled exterior of the house to the backyard. "I think that's the point," I murmured.

"What?"

"Nothing."

I was getting tired of listening to all his complaints and grumbles about stuff neither of us could change.

Not that I'd want to. And maybe that was the real problem. Abuela Gloria was the best! She took care of people, and she made the best food, and she was just so . . . *unique*. Who else's grandmother used to have a pet raccoon? Who else's grandmother spent one spring touring Route 66 with a bunch of motorcyclists? Who else's grandmother was a massive pro wrestling fan? One time, when she was visiting, she took Cristina, Manny, and me to a Royal Rumble. She got us seats so good, one of the bad guys actually glared at Abuela for her loud heckling.

Manny and Cristina and I knew that Abuela would always have our backs if we wanted to do anything out of the ordinary. How could Abuelo have so many complaints about her?

I thought about this as I skimmed leaves off the pool, until an answer came to me. "Maybe she's your unfinished business," I said.

"Eh? No. We've been finished for years. My unfinished business is for you to follow in my footsteps."

I winced. "Um, about that . . . I'm not too sure that's going to happen."

"What?" he demanded as I went inside to get Iggy for a drag around the street. "What do you mean?"

"I don't know if you've been keeping track, but I've bombed two band auditions. I've got one more chance tomorrow, but I'm probably going to blow that one too." I held up a hand to cut short his but-you-are-a-Ramírez speech and added, "Don't get me wrong, I'll try my best. But if I'm honest, getting taken out of band and doing something where I don't have to humiliate myself in front of forty other kids every day actually doesn't sound so bad."

"¿Qué? You can't! My entrance to the afterlife depends on you becoming a great trumpet player!"

I stiffened. It seemed unfair for the afterlife to put that on me, when I really couldn't do any better.

As I pulled Iggy out to the sidewalk, I said, "I already promised to try. What else do you want from me?"

"A star does not simply *try*, mi nieto. A star does not

accept anything less than success. They commit to greatness. They—"

He straightened and gasped.

My breath caught. Was he having another heart attack?

Wait, no. I was pretty sure you needed a beating heart to have a heart attack.

"Abuelo, what's wrong?"

"I'm outside the house! I'm . . . I'm even off the property! I haven't been able to step foot outside the house since I died!"

I looked around. Somehow, I'd been so caught up—or more accurately, *annoyed*—by Abuelo's mood that I hadn't noticed. "Huh."

Abuelo marveled at his street as if he'd never seen a more beautiful sight. To be fair, it was one of the prettiest stretches I'd come across in Miami so far, with a slightly winding road and a canopy of trees shading the drive like nature-made umbrellas.

"It must be that I can leave, but only as long as I'm with you." He tried to pat me, slipping his hand right through my shoulder. I stared at the spot, willing myself not to be creeped out.

"You see?" he said. "This proves it! My unfinished business is tied to you. My job is to make you a star!"

I chewed my lip.

"In fact," Abuelo added, "this gives me an idea!"

"What?" I asked, narrowing my eyes. I hoped his idea wasn't another crazy wardrobe makeover.

"You'll see!"

Why did I think I wasn't going to like this?

♪ ♫ ♩ ♪

I HAD THOUGHT school couldn't possibly get worse. I had thought wrong.

"Now, remember," said Abuelo, keeping pace easily as though he were not in a crowded hallway, walking through oblivious kids as though *they* were invisible to *him,* "you have to *believe* you are a star. Stand tall. Make eye contact. Command the room."

I took a tired breath. We had been up late last night, working on my playing until Mami pounded on the door, telling me to knock it off and go to sleep. Well, *I* was tired from last night. If Abuelo even needed sleep, I'd seen no sign of it.

"Speaking of that, I can't believe you have decided to dress like a . . . a . . . like a *nobody* once again!"

"Will. You. Stop. Talking?"

I glared to my left . . . at a pair of girls standing by an open locker. One of them, a blond girl I recognized from my social studies class, rolled her eyes and said, "Whatever, Eggplantio."

I wasn't even wearing Abuelo's clothes today, but still the

nickname had stuck. And now here Abuelo was, finding even more ways to make me an outcast.

I didn't bother trying to explain—what would I have said? I just looked away and picked up my pace.

A familiar voice called out. "Benny!"

"¡Ay mira! There's that nice girl you like!"

I glanced ahead and spotted Andrea heading my way. She was actually wearing pink for once—a flamingo-colored long-sleeve shirt covered in black bat silhouettes, with combat boots in a matching pattern.

We found an empty bit of wall where we could pull out of the human current, and I relaxed a little bit.

"Are you okay, B? You seem kind of . . . intense."

I shrugged. "Guess I'm nervous about my audition."

"What have I been telling you, mi nieto?" Abuelo said. "Superstars don't ever admit to being nervous!"

I looked away from him, hoping to avoid any more embarrassing missteps, but then I caught myself. Why bother pretending? I'd already shared my big secret with Andrea.

"And, uh, my grandfather came to school with me. For moral support."

She took a half step back, her eyes widening. "He's here? Like, right now?" She reached out a hand, waving it in the space around me like she was petting an invisible dog.

My heartbeat picked up again. I forgot that while I didn't have to worry about Andrea making fun of me, I *did* have to worry about what kind of other attention she might attract.

"Ooh! I feel a cold spot right here!" She waved her hand to the left of me. "He's here, isn't he?"

On my right, Abuelo leaned over to get a better look at the spot where she was gesturing.

"Um, yeah," I said to her. "More or less."

She jumped—literally jumped—and squealed, "I *knew* it!"

I glanced around. Across the hallway, one boy nudged another and murmured something, making them both laugh. Closer to us, a teacher stared, and a girl rolled her eyes at the display. Somehow, an actual real-live ghost drew less attention at this school than Andrea Wade.

"Anyway, I'd better go," I said, rushing the words out. "I don't want too many people around when I get there."

"Break a leg," she said, still staring at the spot on my left.

WHEN I GOT to Mr. Edwards's room, he was sitting at his desk. The air left my lungs. No last-second reprieve today. Here went nothing.

I tapped on the open door, and he stood up. "Benny! Come on in!" He took in my jeans and LA Dodgers T-shirt and nodded. "Looking more like your own person," he said approvingly. "Now, don't you feel better, kiddo?"

I nodded automatically, but when I thought about it, I realized I was actually a little more scared to do this in my own clothes. I mean, sure, wearing Abuelo's clothes had attracted a lot of attention, but it had been like I was wearing a costume. It had felt easier to do something crazy like trying to play the trumpet. Now when Mr. Edwards watched me play, he would be seeing . . . me. Maybe Abuelo knew what he was talking about after all.

"Great!" said Mr. Edwards, settling on a stool by his podium. He gestured at my trumpet case. "Let's get to it!" My breakfast threatened to come up, and I took a couple of deep breaths through my mouth. There was no way this was going to go well.

"Piece of cake!" said Abuelo. "Show the man what a natural talent sounds like!" As I opened up the case and took out his trumpet, I endured a steady stream of reminders and advice, with constant reassurances that he believed in me and knew I would hit this one out of the park.

Last night Abuelo had—finally!—given me some pointers that didn't have to do with how to dress or do my hair or walk. Now, in the band room, I positioned my hands like he taught me, stood tall, and took a deep breath. Abuelo believed in me. If he thought I was a real trumpet player, then I had to be a real trumpet player.

Within a few seconds of pressing the mouthpiece up against my lips and blowing, I knew better. I could not learn in one lesson what every other kid here had been doing for years.

On the other hand, my sound had progressed from farting elephant to sobbing hippo, so clearly, I was improving.

Abuelo ran his fingers through his hair as he heard me "playing," his jaw open in a pained grimace.

"No!" he cried out. "Your third finger goes *here*!" He pointed and I tried to adjust, but it was like somebody had rewired my body, or maybe I wasn't coordinated enough to blow and move my fingers at the same time.

"Blow from the diaphragm!" Abuelo yelled. I had no idea what that meant. I only knew one way to blow, and that was from my mouth.

"Posture!" he roared, and I practically launched the trumpet into the air from trying to make my spine steel-bar straight.

In front of me, Mr. Edwards winced. He drew in a breath, and I was pretty sure he was getting ready to cut me off.

"Ay, never mind," said Abuelo. "I'll do this myself!"

He was standing beside me, and my eyes were on Mr. Edwards, so I couldn't quite see what was happening, but suddenly Abuelo wasn't next to me anymore. I could still sense that he was around, though.

And that's when ... something happened. It felt like ... like I had an instant fever, and my skin was too tight, and then suddenly the notes I was playing were a wrinkled bedsheet that was ironing itself out in front of my eyes. The notes were flowing through me, the music was flowing through me, and it felt smooth, and it felt *good*. I wasn't *playing* music, I *was* music.

The sound must have drifted down the hallway, because some of the other kids in the band poked their heads in the door and stepped inside, staring at me. Everybody seemed to stop what they were doing, as though they'd been handed tickets to the hottest concert of their lives.

Which they kind of had.

Somewhere along the way, I seamlessly transitioned from the B-flat scale Mr. Edwards had asked for into a riff on "Miami Maravilloso." I'd heard that tune so many times, I almost felt like I could play it—and now, somehow, I could. Finally, and too soon, I came to the end. Everybody remained silent at first, but before I could ask if I'd done something wrong, a deafening applause shook the room. They were clapping . . . for me!

I took a step backward, trying to understand what had just happened.

Mr. Edwards hopped up from behind his podium and hurried to my side. "I knew it!" he said. "You really are a chip off the old block! Maybe you had to work through something to find your comfort zone. Maybe it was just a new-school thing, I don't know." He patted my back. "But you did it! And I'm glad I didn't give up on you, kiddo!"

"Uh, thanks," I said, looking around for Abuelo. Where was he?

"There's an audition next month for a student brass quartet. You should try out! If you play like you just did here, you'll be a shoo-in!"

I bit my lip. I hadn't done this. I knew that. But everybody was congratulating me and telling me how terrific my solo was and . . . I liked it. Playing the music had felt amazing too. I had no idea it could be like that.

Then something seemed to . . . *pull,* like I was a bubble splitting into two bubbles, and then I watched Abuelo step *out of* me, as though he were stepping through a door. As though, a few minutes ago, he had disappeared into a room, and the room was me.

He . . . had been . . . inside me. Playing the music. Controlling me.

I mean, I knew, right? I knew it hadn't been me playing. But here was proof.

My breaths shortened and seemed to come quicker. He had controlled me, like a puppet. I struggled to keep from freaking out.

Abuelo held his hands out in front of him, a giant grin on his face. "Now, *that's* how you play the trumpet! That felt amazing!" He beamed at me. "You see?"

I blinked. What was it that he thought I should see? That *he* could play the trumpet?

"Um, sure."

Mr. Edwards laughed. "Um, sure? Kiddo, don't sound so enthusiastic! That brass quartet is a high honor!"

"Sorry," I replied hastily. "It sounds awesome. I was just . . . in the zone, I guess. I don't always think straight after I play like that."

"Oh, of course! Totally understandable!"

"Well," said Abuelo, brushing his hands together. "My work here is done." Then he disappeared. I had no idea where he had gone, but I was pretty sure it wasn't back into me, which was a relief.

I thought I had been just bluffing about being in the zone, but the next few hours really were a blur. Did I go to class? Did I walk from room to room like a ghost? I guess I must have done everything I was supposed to, but I remembered none of it—I was too distracted remembering what it felt like to have Abuelo's music flowing through me.

On my way to lunch, I saw Cristina in the hallway, surrounded by a half dozen girls and a couple of boys. At least she was making friends faster than Manny. I hurried over to tell her about my audition—would she even believe me? She wouldn't need to, though. I had a feeling news of my Ignacio-Ramírez-inspired performance would pass through the school as quickly as the news of my flop audition had. Still, I wanted her to hear it from me.

Except, when I got close, I realized she wasn't simply hanging out with a crowd of friends. They seemed to be trying to talk her up, touching her on the arm and stuff, like she needed consoling.

I wove my way through the circle of kids. "What's going on?" I asked. "Is something wrong?"

"*Everything* is wrong! The cast list is out."

"So? I thought you already knew you weren't going to be the Sugarplum Fairy."

"I did. But I'm not playing Dewdrop either. I got cast as a dancing mouse, Benny!"

"All the parts are good, Cristina," one girl said. "Everybody here was a star at their old school."

"There are no small parts," one of the boys quoted, "only small players."

That did not actually sound all that supportive to me, but Cristina nodded like she was trying to take it to heart.

Turning to me, she said, "I'm sorry, Benny. I know you've got your own stuff to worry about. Is your morning going all right?"

I took a breath to answer but didn't know what to say. Dancing *mattered* to Cristina. If I had flopped my audition, it wouldn't have hurt me nearly as much. And it wasn't fair, because unlike me with the trumpet, Cristina worked hard at dance. She didn't have some prima ballerina to take over and do her pirouettes for her.

Before I could find the right words, Manny slinked by, sniffing at lockers and grinning at anybody who looked at him for too long.

Somewhere behind me, a kid murmured, "Here, kitty kitty," and someone else laughed. For a moment, a grimace flew across Manny's face. An instant later it was gone, but I'd seen it. For him to break character like that was big.

"Hi, uh, Cheshy," I said. I didn't ask about his day. I didn't need to.

"Benny! Maravilloso! Are you going to the cafeteria?" someone called.

I caught sight of the voice's source on the other side of Manny—Aaron, a big kid who played the kettledrum.

Was he calling *me* Maravilloso? Like Abuelo's song?

"Um, yeah?" I answered.

"You should come sit with us!"

That's when I realized he was walking with a whole crowd of band kids.

"Yeah!" said DeSean. "Come hang out with us, Maravilloso!"

His face split in a giant grin, and I noticed that he had navy-blue rubber bands in his braces. He was a trumpet player like me, so I wondered if it hurt to press his lips up against the mouthpiece with braces.

"Man," he added, "that was something this morning! I did *not* see that coming!" DeSean was either the second or third trumpet player, depending on where I sat, so I was a little surprised to see him taking my success so well. I wondered if I would be as nice if I were in his shoes.

"I did," said Aaron. "I totally saw it coming."

His claim was met with a chorus of groans and at least one kid saying "Liar!"

"I'm serious!" Turning back to me, he added, "I figured you were nervous, but I knew music had to run in your family!"

"I don't even mind losing first chair if I get to hear you play like that up close!" I hadn't noticed that Harold, who'd gotten moved out of first chair the day of my first audition, was part of the group.

Cristina nudged me, a questioning look on her face. "Benny . . . ?"

"Oh my God, bro, did you actually manage to play the trumpet?" Manny stared at me, all signs of the Cheshire Cat gone.

"Uh . . . I mean . . ." How could I make this make sense to him, when he *knew* I'd never played before this week? "Yeah, I played. It wasn't a big deal, though. I just, uh, managed to—"

DeSean thumped my arm. "What? Man, stop being modest." Turning to Manny, he added, "It was just the best solo I've ever heard. No big deal, though."

Aaron pulled my elbow. "Come on, Maravilloso! If we don't hurry, the line'll get long!"

I glanced at Manny and Cristina, who were both staring at me, their faces scrunched in total confusion.

"Um, I'll tell you about it later," I said to Manny and Cristina. "I've got to . . . I'm gonna go with my friends."

Was this what it was like for them *all* the time? Just . . . being good at something and getting admired for it? Well, not right now, but before this week?

It was kind of awesome.

I followed Aaron, DeSean, and the other band kids into

the cafeteria and sat at their table, soaking up the company and the praise. From the corner of my eye, I saw Andrea sitting at our usual table, but I avoided looking directly at her. It's not like it was mandatory that we sit together or anything, but I knew she'd be giving me the same confused stare Manny and Cristina had a minute ago. I wasn't ready to let that ruin my moment in the sun.

But my sunbathing was short-lived. At the next table over sat a different crowd of kids, and I recognized some of the ones who had been consoling Cristina earlier. They were crowding around a girl I didn't know, and I wondered if this was the girl she'd talked so much about, Sarah.

I frowned.

As badly as I'd wanted to join one of the loud, fun tables earlier this week, now that I was here, all I could think about was Cristina and Manny, and how some of the guys I was sitting with today had been calling me Eggplantio Ramírez just yesterday. They were talking about my solo this morning and kept trying to include me in the conversation, but I could only muster a smile here and there and two- or three-word answers.

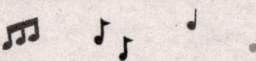

I DIDN'T see Abuelo again the rest of the day. It must be tiring to hijack a body.

I wasn't sure how I felt about not having him around,

though. I guess it was a relief to find that once he was out of the house, he didn't have to stick to my side like glue. It was nice not having him constantly telling me how to act or how to be a *star* or whatever. On the other hand, the only people in my life who actually knew what was going on were him and Andrea, and I hadn't seen either of them since the audition. The truth? I was starting to get worried.

What if he'd tried to go home without me and had gotten lost? As far as I knew, he didn't have some kind of ghostly GPS giving him directions to the school. How exactly did Abuelo travel from place to place when he disappeared and reappeared, anyway? Did it take him longer to go to places that were farther away? For all his talking about his life, I realized I didn't know much about how his death worked.

When I finally got home and went upstairs to change out of my school clothes, I found him in my room. He stood in the middle of the floor, ankle-deep in clutter, staring at the ceiling with his arms wide open.

"What are you doing, Abuelo?"

"Isn't it obvious? Now that I have completed my unfinished business, I'm waiting to be taken to the afterlife."

My eyes bulged so hard it felt like they might pop. "What?"

"Esteban said he would come for me on New Year's Eve, but that's only because he underestimated the great Ignacio Ramírez! He didn't expect me to fix your life so quickly!"

I took a step back. "You . . . think you fixed my life?"

He frowned and faced me again. "Yes, of course! You are a star at school, your wardrobe has improved cien por ciento—or at least it had until today. And your hair is perfect! What else can you ask for?"

When had I asked for *any* of those things?

"Anyway," Abuelo went on more quietly, "it wouldn't hurt for me to get out of here before Gloria arrives."

I stared at him. The silence dragged on, like Abuelo expected me to agree that his work here was done. We stood there for an hour or maybe just a minute, but a *long* minute, and then Abuelo said, "I wonder why Samuel hasn't come yet."

My forehead pulsed. At first, I wondered if I was starting to get one of the migraines Mami sometimes got. But then I realized I was just angry. "Well, for starters, you haven't 'fixed' a single thing!"

"What? How can you say that?" He reached out to pat me on the head—or tried to. "Ay, mi nieto, I get it. I know you will be heartbroken when I leave, after these days we have spent making you a success, but always be glad for this time." He turned his eyes to the light fixture and again stretched his arms out at his sides, like getting into the afterlife depended on how good his posture was.

I sighed. "Look, don't get me wrong. Back in Mr. Edwards's room, that was the most amazing feeling. But that was *you* playing, not me. So what happens when I have to show up for class tomorrow? Or if they stick me in that brass quartet he told me about? I'll just be no-talent Benny

Ramírez again, whose trumpet-playing sounds like garbage?"

He blinked a couple of times, like it genuinely had not occurred to him that there would be a tomorrow for me, whether or not he got called up to that great fiesta in the sky. And then his shoulders slumped. "Oh."

"Yeah," I agreed.

I sat heavily on the bed. We needed a plan B.

Just then a musical car horn sounded from outside, playing the refrain from "Guantanamera." I shot back to my feet and stepped over a pile of clutter, toward the balcony door. I saw Cristina emerge onto the balcony through her own door. She looked toward the gate and gasped.

"Guess who's here?"

I didn't need to guess, though, because I knew who it was. Only one person in my life had a horn that made that sound.

I joined Cristina on the balcony as the automatic gate opened and a food truck pulled into the driveway. Stenciled on the truck's side was GLORIA'S CABANA CUBANA.

Abuela Gloria had arrived ahead of schedule.

CHAPTER NINE

Cristina turned and bolted, and I crossed our connected balcony to follow through her room, which had fewer tripping hazards than mine. At the landing, Manny joined us in a dangerous sprint down the stairs.

At the bottom, we all almost plowed into Mami. She leaned against the door, hand on the knob, one corner of her blouse untucked and sticking out of her slacks.

"Your mother is here," she said to Papi, her voice flat.

"I know."

"She was supposed to come Saturday."

Papi nodded. "I know."

"We're not ready."

"It'll be okay."

"This is why you shouldn't have invited her," Abuelo said. "You give that woman an inch, she'll take half the residual income from your first record!"

I tensed at his appearance, but of course nobody else noticed.

Mami took a breath, then tugged the door open. "Gloria!" she cried out, seemingly delighted.

"Luisa! Félix!" Abuela stood in the door like some kind of female Santa Claus, with a big belly, canvas bags hanging from her shoulders, arms spread out, and a booming voice. Except Abuela Gloria's hair was solid black. And she didn't have a beard.

Cristina, Manny, and I crowded around Abuela, welcoming and hugging her. Everybody seemed to have forgotten their problems for the moment—Manny wasn't even a cat anymore.

Once the group hug broke up, Abuela stepped into the foyer, and Cristina, Manny, and I took her bags. She placed her now-free hands on her hips and surveyed the entrance. "So . . . this is the palace that Ignacio's music bought."

I nodded. "Isn't it amazing?"

She looked at me and her expression softened. "It's certainly impressive," she acknowledged. "But maybe un poquito tacky."

"I'm rewriting my will!" Abuelo cried out. "That woman is *not allowed*! Bring me a pen!"

Abuela's gaze traveled upward, taking in the lofted foyer and finally resting on the portrait of Abuelo hanging at the top of the stairs. She turned back toward me. "Ay, Benicio, I wish you could've seen the little house we had in Miami Beach. It was tiny, yes. Just plugging in the hair dryer would make the power go out. But we were happy. Bigger isn't always better."

I tried to imagine a time before Abuelo was a star. The two of them had divorced before I was born, so I had no memories of them together. When we visited Florida, we would stay with Abuela in Tampa, where she had opened a Cuban restaurant. In the early afternoon, before the dinner crowd, she would let me taste dishes she was experimenting with, before she added them to the menu. She really seemed to listen to what I thought, even if I said something silly like *It needs more M&M's, Abuela!* One time, when I was five, she actually added M&M's to her arroz con picadillo just for me. It wasn't bad, honestly.

"I wish I could have seen it, Abuela." What I really wished was that I could have seen them together.

"It was a hole," Abuelo muttered from somewhere behind me. "Ancient and falling apart. No place for a rising star!"

I stiffened and made a cut-it-out motion with my hand, behind my back where I hoped only he could see it.

We led Abuela into the living room. She picked the purple sequined shirt up from where I had flung it across the alligator sculpture. "Apparently, Ignacio left you a lot of work to do, if his clothes are still draped all over the place."

"Oh, no, that's Benny's," Cristina said helpfully.

Abuela raised her eyebrows and peered at me.

"It's . . . ah . . . important to have a style when you go to an arts school," I said.

She nodded slowly, a gesture that somehow managed to not look like agreement. Turning back to the rest of the family, she said, "Bueno, Luisa, have you all eaten yet?"

"Ah, we were just getting ready to pull something together."

Getting ready to call for delivery, more likely.

"Well, don't you worry about a thing," Abuela said. She pointed at the bag Manny held and said, "I brought some groceries, and I have a truck full of cooking implements. Let me whip something up." Turning back to me, she added, "Benicio, do you want to be my taste tester, like the old times?"

"Sure!"

I took the supplies from Manny and led Abuela to the kitchen. Abuelo followed us both, sulking, but quiet, at least. While I poured myself a glass of orange juice, Abuela pulled what seemed like a restaurant's worth of cookware and ingredients out of the bag.

Within five minutes, Abuela had a pot heating up with the ingredients of her famous stew, a cross between ropa vieja and ajiaco cubano, filled with flank steak, corn, yuca, and plantains. Once she got the mix bubbling, she shuffled through the handful of utensils Abuelo left—one spatula, a strainer, and a potato masher—and said, "It's worse than I thought. I guess I need to make another trip to the truck. Can you keep an eye on the stew for me? Just stir it every once in a while."

She was gone before I finished saying "You bet!"

When Abuela had decided she'd rather spend time with her family than waste it dealing with staff and landlords, she'd closed her restaurant down and bought the food truck as a kind of semi-retirement. But great cooking is great cooking, and her food truck was as in-demand as her restaurant ever was. It was always mobbed everywhere she took it, and it even showed up on "best of" lists for food trucks.

I stood close to the stove, savoring the aroma of the flank steak and scallions. Abuelo stood beside me and made a show of inhaling as well, and then said to me, "¿Cómo huele, mi nieto?"

I looked up at him. "You can't smell it?"

He shook his head. "I hadn't really missed it until now. But I will say one thing for Gloria—in all my travels throughout Latin America and the rest of the world, I never met a better cook. Take a deep breath for both of us, Benny."

I turned back to the pot and did as he said, doing my best to take a double-sized whiff. My mouth watered and

I resisted the temptation to conduct a taste test. "It's amazing," I said, not sure if it was what he wanted to hear or if I was making it worse.

I took a sip from my juice and swallowed wrong. Desperate to not cough all over the pot, I turned my face quickly into my elbow—and ended up spilling half a glass of OJ into the stew.

"¡Cuidado!" Abuelo cried.

I stared at the pot. *No!* I had ruined dinner. And I hadn't just ruined *any* dinner. I had ruined Abuela's specialty.

I grabbed the serving spoon, but there was no way to spoon out the juice. It had already mixed in.

"What a waste!" Abuelo said mournfully.

I pulled a smaller spoon out of the drawer and tasted the stew. It wasn't *bad*, precisely, but it was *off*, and not in a good way. And it definitely wasn't Abuela's famous stew.

"Maybe I can fix it," I said, looking frantically around our mostly empty kitchen.

"You can't fix this, mi nieto! I've heard what happens when you improvise! And you *definitely* don't want to make Gloria angry!"

I poked through Abuela's canvas bags, my mind racing. Something to take away flavor. What could work? Something bland, starchy, absorbent. More potatoes would be perfect, but she had only brought with her what she planned to use. I ran to the fridge, trying to think of other alternatives. Mushrooms. Carrots. Maybe even peas, which I hated. Normally, we would have some of these things, but of course right now all we had was leftovers. Abuela would definitely notice a slice of cold pepperoni pizza floating around in her stew.

There was a bag of frozen corn in the freezer, but it would take several minutes to heat up, and Abuela would surely be back by then. Also, there was no corn in Abuela's stew. Everybody knew that.

"I think you're right," I said, searching through the fridge.

And then my eyes landed on some packets of pizza toppings. Bacon bits. Crushed red pepper. Parmesan cheese. Also a couple of packets of honey from a takeout Chinese food order.

They might help.

I grabbed the bundle and ripped several open.

"Benny, no!" Abuelo cried out. But the meal was definitely wrecked if I did nothing. All of these flavors could at least balance the citrusy tang. I stirred quickly, willing my additions to dissolve.

I held the last bit of crushed red pepper, debating whether it would push the meal into unpleasantly spicy territory.

"*Benicio Ignacio Ramírez!* ¿Qué tú crees que estás haciendo?"

I froze at the sound of Abuela's angry voice, unable to remember how to make words. I considered tossing the packets I still held into the trash, but it was too late.

Abuela stood beside me. "I said you could help me *test* the food, but you should know better than to *tamper* with an artist's work!"

Next to her, Abuelo *mm-hmm*ed loudly. "¿Qué te dije? I am so happy it's not me."

I swallowed. "I'm sorry, Abuela. I accidentally spilled juice in the pot. There was no way to take it out, so I hoped maybe I could fix it."

Abuela frowned. "Well, accidents happen. Let's see what the damage is." She took a clean spoon, stirred the stew up a bit, and tasted it.

Her eyes widened and I winced. I had ruined it for sure.

"Benicio . . . this is terrific! What did you add?"

I showed her the empty packets and explained my reasoning.

Her eyes lit up. "That was brilliant, mi vida! The honey you put in balanced out the acidity of the juice. The bacon added salt, which also balanced the flavor. And the crushed pepper . . ." She kissed her lips. "That added *zing*! This is magnificent! Your instincts . . . you must have inherited them from me!"

Abuelo took a step back. "¿Qué?"

I felt so light I could have lifted right off the ground. "You mean I didn't sabotage dinner?"

"Benicio, you should let me give you some real cooking lessons while I'm here. With your instincts and my experience, you could be an amazing cook! What do you think—would you like that?"

"No, he would not," said Abuelo, wagging his finger in her direction. "My grandson needs to practice the trumpet, so that he can be a star and I can get into the afterlife!"

I wrung my hands together. "I don't have any instincts, Abuela. I just used what I could find! I got lucky." I pointed at the pot. "My real talent is making disasters, like spilling the juice in the first place."

I forced a laugh, but Abuela just stared at me, a sad look on her face.

"Um, anyway, I'll get bowls," I said. "Good thing you brought some." I pointed at the deep white bowls Abuela had lugged in with the rest of the kitchen utensils, now stacked neatly on the counter, only to discover I was still holding the ladle. I tried to drop it back in the pan but fumbled it. As the ladle clattered off the stove and down to the kitchen floor, I grabbed for it and succeeded instead in slapping it across the room, spilling globs of stew all over the tile.

"Heh. See what I mean?" I reached for the paper towels. Before I was anywhere close to the mess, though, Iggy had slid across the room like a runner sprinting for second base. I watched, stunned, as he slurped up the dribbles I had scattered.

"I can't believe it!" I said. "That's the first thing Iggy's really gone after since we've been here!" I pointed to Iggy's regular kibble bowl. "Normally, it takes him more than a day to work through a single meal!"

Abuela poured a tiny bit of the stew over the kibble, and Iggy went after it with gusto.

"His name is Iggy?" Abuela asked, her brow furrowed.

I nodded.

"Well, he doesn't seem to agree with you, when it comes to your abilities. And neither do I. We can begin cooking lessons tomorrow!"

WHEN WE SAT down to eat, Abuela gave me so much credit, you'd think I cooked the whole meal from scratch. Mami and Papi both joined in when they tasted the stew, calling out the flavors of the citrus and the pepper and the honey. Cristina *mmmm*ed loudly, and even Manny made a sound that might have been a purr.

Abuelo paced between the dining room and the hall, and I wondered if he was frustrated because he couldn't see for himself whether Abuela was overselling my accidental contribution.

For a while, it felt like old times. Then Abuela shifted in her seat. "So why doesn't everybody tell me about all the exciting things you're doing now? I can't wait to hear about school and the new jobs!"

"It's fine, I guess," Cristina said.

I debated whether I wanted to talk about my trumpet-playing. Would that be an unwelcome reminder of her ex? Also, it wasn't like it was really *my* trumpet-playing. *Hey, Abuela, I've got everybody fooled into thinking I'm an amazing musician!* The moment the thought occurred to me, I knew I'd be keeping band to myself.

"Benny's already made some friends," Mami said, "and, uh, I'm learning a lot about grading and lesson plans and seating charts and 'positive behavior support.'"

"Manny too," Papi chimed in. "He got a big part in the upcoming show!"

Manny made a sound that might possibly have been a hiss.

"Ooh, tell me all about it!"

Manny, Cristina, and I just stared at one another, each willing somebody else to go first.

Abuela frowned. "You're usually all so excited to talk about your days! What's really going on?"

Papi sighed. "I'm sure everything's fine," he said. "We all just have a lot of new things to adjust to."

"It's been hectic," said Mami.

"Why hectic?" Abuela asked.

Mami sighed. "Since we have this big house now, I thought it would help us become a part of the SMPAS family faster if I offered to host the school New Year's Eve party.

It's months away, but I'm starting to wonder if we'll still be living out of suitcases and boxes!"

A party? Here?

"Maybe it's not too late to back out," Papi said.

Mami gave a little head shake. She wasn't the type to back out once she said she would do something.

"That does sound stressful," Abuela said. "Maybe you need to do something fun to take your mind off it. Oh! That reminds me!" She turned toward Papi. "Félix, I saw a new show that you would just love. It's about an artist who makes magical murals that let people live life in somebody else's shoes, and it reminded me so much of the sort of stories you tell. It's by Felipe Maldonado. Didn't you used to work with him?"

Papi seemed to clench his jaw for a second, then he slowly relaxed, like he had to force himself to smile. "Yes, I did. I'm so glad the show is doing well."

Something clicked in my head: This had to be the show Papi had left. Or was fired from. But . . . if the show actually made it to production, why did Abuela say it was by Felipe Maldonado? Why wasn't Papi's name on the show?

Abuelo stopped his pacing and paused right by the table, frowning. Maybe he noticed the change in Papi's demeanor too.

Abuela's eyebrows knitted together. "Eh, what about you, Manuel? How is your acting going?"

Manny meowed several times.

Abuelo made a face. "¿Qué pasa con este niño?"

"Eh, Manny, are you a cat?" Abuela asked, her head cocked.

Papi jumped in. "Manny is an actor who really commits to his roles, and right now he's playing the Cheshire Cat, so . . ." He waved his hands, like that was all the explanation anybody could need.

Abuela placed her fork beside her plate. "Well, that's all good, Manuel, but I came to visit my grandchildren. At the dinner table, you need to come as yourself. No cats allowed."

Manny shrugged and stopped sniffing at his plate but didn't say anything.

Abuela sighed dramatically. "Cristina!" she said, turning her way. "I know *you* will have something to tell me! How is your dancing coming along?"

Cristina threw her fork down. "The fashion design class is making costumes for the show, and they want us to get fitted on Monday. As if it's not insulting enough to be cast as a mouse, they want me to be measured for it by one of my classmates? So that everybody can participate in my humiliation! Well, they can forget it! I'm not doing it!"

The last words came out as a sob, and Cristina lowered her face into her hands.

Mami reached out to her, but before she could touch her shoulder, Cristina wailed, "I'm quitting dance!"

"Dios mío," said Abuelo. "What is happening?"

Papi leaned in. "You don't want to do that. You love to dance!"

"What are you talking about?" Mami asked. "My goodness, I've been so focused on the house, I didn't even realize you were so unhappy!"

Abuela put a hand on Cristina's. "Ay, pobrecita, I'm so sorry you're having a bad time. I know how much you love dancing. But it's okay to take a break sometimes and gather yourself."

Abuelo roared. "¿Qué? Nonsense!" He leaned over the table and pointed, as if Cristina could see or hear him. "You are a Ramírez! Ramírezes do not quit, they do not 'take a break'! The show must go on!"

I rolled my eyes. Again with his *You are a Ramírez* speech. Couldn't he see that being a Ramírez was no free ticket to success?

Abuelo turned to Abuela Gloria. "This is *your* fault!"

"That makes zero sense."

Cristina glanced up at me, and it was only then I realized I'd spoken out loud.

"Don't act surprised, Benny," Cristina said. "I've told you every single day how miserable I've been. But I guess you're too caught up in being a band star to notice."

"That's not fair," I said. "I have totally had your back every time you—"

I stopped. Was this true? I *had* been pretty focused on myself the past few days.

"Sure you have, *Maravilloso*," she retorted.

Abuelo leaned over the table toward Abuela. "You never supported my dreams, and now here you are, encouraging your granddaughter to give up on hers too! And not just the girl—you want my grandson to take up cooking when heaven itself has sent me to make him a musician!"

I flailed my hands in a shushing motion.

"What are you doing?" Cristina asked.

"Uh . . ." I glanced down at my plate. "There was a fly!"

"Your art is supposed to bring you joy," Abuela added. "If it isn't, it's no crime to stop for a little while."

Abuelo's eyes widened so much that I wondered if a ghost could pop a vein. Finally, he blew an impressively long raspberry at her—a raspberry worthy of a megastar trumpet player.

"Cut it out!" I shouted. "And put your tongue back in your mouth!"

Suddenly it was very quiet at the table.

A tingle swept from my chest to my face as I noticed all the eyes now pointed at me.

"Uh . . . Iggy!" I said. "Quit begging!" I glanced around the table. "He really shouldn't be begging for scraps." I stood and walked over to him. "I'll take care of it."

I tugged Iggy—who definitely preferred to be by the table—toward the kitchen. Meeting Abuelo's gaze, I gestured with my head in a move I hoped might be mistaken for natural, urging him to follow me.

At the table, the conversation resumed, a bit more quietly. "I'm not sure it's possible for Cristina to drop a class 'for a little while,'" Mami said. "It's a grade."

"But, Mami, can't you do something? Please?" Cristina begged.

"Do you see now?" Abuelo asked as we both left their view—well, technically only *I* did, since they couldn't see him anyway.

"See what?"

He glared. "Do you see how that woman made me feel guilty for following my dreams, and now she's encouraging her grandchildren to give up on theirs?"

"This isn't her fault! None of this is new." I was whispering, but hopefully he could hear my annoyance.

He went on as if I hadn't said anything. "This is why I couldn't stay with her! And now your family wants to bring her here, into my house, when I can't get away! I can't! I can't stay here!"

"Calm down!"

"I have to find a way to get ahold of, um, Osvaldo!" Abuelo turned around, searching dramatically as though he might find his deceased drummer in the kitchen somewhere if he just looked hard enough. Then his attention landed on me. "You have to help me. You can vouch for how well you are doing now! They have to let me in!"

My ears pounded as I listened to this. "Are you kidding? You can't leave! Everything's a mess! Cristina just quit dancing, Manny thinks he's a cat, and I can only play the trumpet when I'm channeling a dead man!"

Papi's voice startled me, and only then did I realize that at some point I had gone from angry whispering to angry shouting. "Hey, Benny? Who are you talking to?"

"I . . ." I glanced at Iggy, but there was no way anybody would believe I was lecturing the dog.

Manny's face appeared in the entry. "Bro, are you talking to yourself?"

"No seas ridiculo," Mami said. "I'm sure there's a perfectly logical explanation. Right, Benny?"

I walked to where Manny stood. From there I could see Mami . . . and the entire table, done with their arguing and united in wondering what was wrong with me.

"Uh, right!"

They all stared, and it occurred to me that they were waiting for a perfectly logical explanation . . .

"Um, I saw a video online about how, um, when you're trying to figure out how you feel about things, you should imagine you're talking it through with somebody so you can, uh—"

"Bro," said Manny, "you were *arguing*."

"It sounded like you were losing," Cristina chimed in.

"And what's this about a dead man?" Papi asked.

"I . . . uh, a lot of music was written by dead guys, right? So in a sense every time we play something from a long time ago, we're, uh . . ."

Abuela wiped her mouth and dropped her napkin on the table. "That does it! This family needs more help than I realized. I was just going to stay the weekend and help you set things up, but now I see that you need me to stay longer, until everything is back on an even keel!"

Somewhere behind me, Abuelo wailed, "Noooooooo!"

CHAPTER TEN

Saturday morning I woke up before Manny and Cristina—or maybe they were awake and sulking in their rooms. I didn't want to stew by myself in all of Abuelo's old clutter, so I went downstairs and poured myself cereal and enjoyed the first quiet morning since we'd come to Miami. Even Abuelo seemed to be sleeping late today.

Only after I'd finished and rinsed my bowl did I notice that Abuela was already awake in the guestroom. I poked my head in the open door and almost did a double take to see how organized it was—she had completely unpacked the suitcase we'd carried in for her, and Abuelo's stuff was neatly collected into a single corner.

"Wow. I can't believe you're already unpacked. I've been

here a week and still have to walk carefully to keep from tripping over the stuff in my room."

She looked up from the magazine she had been reading. "Buenos días, Benicio. To be fair, you've been busy with school and everything else, while I have no other obligations. Plus, unlike you, I didn't have to move in everything I owned. I only brought enough for a few days."

"I guess that's true. But you made it look so neat in here! The mess seems less . . . messy."

Abuela grinned, as if she was pleased that I had noticed. "When you are running a restaurant—especially when you're doing it out of the back of a truck—it's very important to be organized and know where everything is. After all these years, putting things in order right away is a habit now."

I nodded and stepped into her room, examining the memorabilia in the corner. A bobblehead of Abuelo playing his trumpet caught my eye, down on the bottom shelf and facing the wall as though he were in time-out, but still nodding sadly.

I winced.

Gesturing to the statuette, I said, "That bobblehead was facing out before."

"Mmm? Oh yes, I moved it," she replied absently.

"Wow. You really . . . didn't like Abuelo, huh?"

She hurried by my side and ran a hand through my hair. "Mi cielo, it's not like that at all. I loved him. I don't think I ever stopped loving him, to tell you the truth. I only turned the doll around because . . . well, it's unsettling to have your ex-husband nodding and staring at you all the time while you're trying to make yourself at home!"

If she thought *that* was unsettling, she ought to try having his ghost keeping you up all night talking your ear off.

"Anyway," she continued, gesturing to the memorabilia around her, "this wasn't Ignacio. None of this was. This is all just junk, and it's junk that got in our way. If it were up to me, I'd get rid of it all."

Abuelo chose this moment to come slowly into view. "Of course you would," he said. "You hated everything that reminded you of my success."

I tasted something sour in the back of my throat. I just wanted all the people I loved to get along—why was that so much to ask for?

"Didn't you want Abuelo to live his dream?"

She sighed. "This wasn't his dream, mi vida. His dream was to make music, not to be on cereal boxes. These are the things that pulled him away from his family, until these *objects* split us all up."

"These are the things that paid for our lifestyle!" Abuelo insisted. "We could have had it all! We *did* have it all! And you could have shared this mansion with me!"

I picked up a Miami Maravilloso key chain. "I don't understand. How did being a star take him away from you and Papi? It seems like it would have been fun traveling all over the world and stuff."

"He spent more time filming car-wax commercials than he did sharing meals with his family."

Abuelo threw his hands in the air. "That's not . . . that's not . . . Those commercials paid a lot of money, okay?"

I couldn't tell if he was trying to convince me or trying to talk to her.

"I wish you two could have talked it out while he was alive."

Abuela sank onto the edge of the bed, her shoulders drooping. "Oh, we tried, Benicio. Or rather, *I* tried. But he wasn't listening."

From the living room, Cristina's voice rang out. "Forget it, Mami! I'm not doing it!"

So much for Saturday-morning peace and quiet. It felt like we'd done more shouting and arguing this week than we ever did back in Los Angeles.

"Uh-oh," I said, heading out to investigate.

I barely made it into the living room before Cristina rounded on me. "This is *your* fault, Benny! You and your talking to yourself or imaginary friends or whatever! Now Mami thinks we *all* need to go to a psychologist!" She turned back to Mami and pointed at me. "You should just send *him*!"

Next to her, Manny glared at me.

I looked from one to the other. "Huh?"

Mami held out a hand. "Priya is not a psychologist, she's a counselor, but even if she were, what's wrong with that? Sometimes it's good to talk through the things you're struggling with, and goodness knows we're all struggling right now."

"What's going on?" I asked. "Who are we talking to?"

"A shrink!" Cristina said.

"Ay, Cristina, deja ya." Mami shook her head. "Benny, Priya Shankar is a counselor who works for the school. I was talking to her yesterday and I told her how this move had put a lot of stress on us all, and she offered to make some time for us. She has an opening on her calendar in three weeks. Group sessions. It's incredibly generous of her!"

Manny meowed. Angrily. Yeah, he was very convincing in the totally-not-needing-to-talk-to-a-therapist department.

My stomach knotted up and I took a deep breath to try to steady it. Manny was acting weird, and Cristina was constantly on the verge of tears, but she was right. It was obviously me talking to Abuelo—to "myself"—that brought this on.

"Mami, I promise, I won't do it again."

She crossed to where I stood and put a hand on my shoulder. "Benny, this isn't about you, and it isn't a punishment. It's for everybody. She's not going to talk to *you,* she's going to talk to *us all.*"

Manny hopped onto the sofa and pawed at it as though it were a scratching post. Even without claws, he was going to tear the furniture if he didn't stop, and that would only make things worse.

I grabbed the spray bottle Mami had been using to

clean the dusty lamps. Pointing the bottle at him, I gave it a squeeze. *"Manny, stop it!"*

Manny blinked at me as water dripped down his face. For a second, we all just stared in silence, then he jumped off the sofa and sprinted out to the foyer. Seconds later, I saw him up in the loft. He stared down at me, his eyes wide, and then hurried out of sight.

I chewed my lip. That look he gave me. Manny and I had always been so close, before. When had that changed?

Suddenly it occurred to me that when I'd wanted my own bedroom, I'd promised Manny that we would still spend time together, and we hadn't. I'd been busy learning trumpet, perfecting my "look," and listening to Abuelo's stories about his glory days. Maybe some of this *was* my fault.

Cristina pointed upstairs. "He may be weird, but he's not wrong," she said, and then she stomped away herself.

I tried to remember if Manny had actually said a single word other than *meow*. I guess he couldn't be wrong if he never said anything.

Mami put her arm about me, and for an instant I wondered if it was to keep me from running off too, but she didn't squeeze or anything.

"Benny, Cristina's wrong. This isn't anybody's fault." She pulled away and turned me so she could meet my eyes. "But talking through everything as a family will help, and having somebody keep us focused and asking the right questions will help too. If you get on board, your sister and brother will too."

"Me?" That didn't make sense. Manny liked me as a brother, but I wasn't an artist like he and Cristina were. And Cristina was the oldest. "Why would they care what I think? They're both furious at me."

"Your sister and brother are both temperamental. But you are steady. You're calm and thoughtful. You may not see it, but I do: what you think matters to both of them." She dropped her hands. "Can you be on my side on this?"

I couldn't remember her ever talking to me like that, like she was asking for help. But of course I was on her side—she was my mom. And anyway, having someone to talk out our problems with didn't seem like the worst idea right now.

CHAPTER ELEVEN

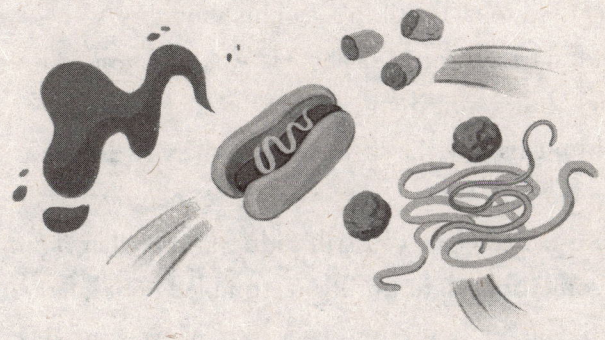

Having a ghost animate your body and show you how to play the trumpet *from the inside* is definitely the best way to learn, and I would recommend it to anybody who gets the chance. But only if your ghost respects boundaries.

In the two weeks or so since my "successful" performance for Mr. Edwards, I had worked out an agreement with Abuelo. He could take over at home and lead me through the things I needed to learn—so no hotdogging, no "Miami Maravilloso." At school, though, he needed to let *me* handle the trumpet.

He was finally seeing that it meant nothing if he played my way into the band and then abandoned me. Instead, our attention was now focused on the brass quartet audition. If he could teach me enough that I could earn a spot on my own, then he was sure he'd be allowed into his heavenly party.

Having him inhabit my body was still weird, but I was getting used to it. I couldn't read his thoughts, so I assumed he couldn't read mine either. He was just controlling my muscles, but I could still feel it. I was learning so much from him this way that it was worth the weirdness.

Abuelo said I was "creating muscle memory," that even with a great teacher, you still didn't know what it *felt* like to do something right until you stumbled on it a few times. Instead, you got nonsense advice like "Move your air faster! But *don't* blow harder!" But with Abuelo's help, I was getting there a lot sooner, because I didn't have to guess what that meant.

Unfortunately, when I flew solo without Abuelo's help, which I tried to do as much as possible, people didn't see how *well* I was playing, they only saw how much *worse* I sounded than that one time I blew their expectations away.

I tried not to think about that as I sat in the band room now, the trumpet pressed to my lips. Mr. Edwards nodded along as I made my way through a section, a hitch in his nod showing where I'd missed a couple of notes. "Okay, okay, that's good, thanks."

I rested Abuelo's trumpet on its stand.

Beside me, DeSean got ready for his turn. In addition to

Harold, the two of us were going to audition for the single trumpet spot in the brass quartet, and we'd been attending before-school practice sessions twice a week to prepare.

Abuelo watched DeSean begin to fill the room with music, and he shook his head. "You should let me take over for you," he told me, somehow audible despite DeSean's high notes trilling right next to me. "You don't need these practices—you receive far better instruction at home from me."

I made a shushing motion, then acted like I was wiping a bit of spit off the horn. Even with Abuelo being a constant distraction, something dawned on me as I watched DeSean's eyes sweep across the measures.

There was one thing "muscle memory" couldn't help with.

"I need every minute of practice I can get if I want to be as good as you at reading the music," I said after DeSean finished.

DeSean beamed his colorful grin. I was improving at saying things to Abuelo that wouldn't sound strange to other people around me.

"You're not the only one, kiddo," said Mr. Edwards. "Still, I'm surprised that, with your talent, your teachers in California didn't push you to sight-read more."

"You had it last Tuesday, though," said DeSean. "It was weird—one minute you were making a bunch of mistakes, and then all of a sudden you were Dizzy Gillespie."

Mr. Edwards nodded. "That's why I think you've got some kind of a block you're working through, like you're not yet comfortable here or something. Because you get these flashes of brilliance."

"Yeah," I agreed. "It's probably nerves. Sometimes I'm better at channeling my grandfather's spirit than others." That was the actual truth, but neither of them would have believed how true it was.

Abuelo was only supposed to take over my playing at home, but once in a while at school it seemed like he got so frustrated with me that he couldn't help himself.

"You know," DeSean said, "when I get nervous, I take a long breath, hold it for as long as I can, and then let it out slowly. It works for me—maybe it'll work for you too."

"Thanks," I said, smiling. I really appreciated how DeSean didn't act like we were competing—we were both just working to improve. He'd been helping me get better all along, giving me pointers on how to read music faster and how to keep my mute from falling out of the horn.

"Don't let your guard down, mi nieto," Abuelo said, almost as though he could read my thoughts. "That boy is not your friend. He's just trying to catch you off guard. Believe me, I've been stabbed in the back before."

I chewed my lip. I was sure the music industry was every bit as competitive as Abuelo said it was, but it made me sad to think that he couldn't even imagine that not everybody was like that. Maybe at next week's counseling session with

Ms. Shankar, I could surreptitiously pick up some ways to make Abuelo less suspicious of everybody.

"I'm begging you, let me take over. Let me blow this upstart out of the water for you. Just once, so he can think about it every time he plays."

I shook my head violently.

"Are you okay, man?" DeSean asked.

"Um, yeah. I was just working out a crick in my neck."

"Well, if you're done," said Mr. Edwards, "then I'd like to hear you both play from measure twenty-four on."

I flipped the music to the right page and waited for the signal. This was a section I had pretty well memorized, so my reading didn't have to be perfect—it was just good to keep my eyes on the notes to remind myself where the music went. And honestly, I had gotten to the point where even without Abuelo playing, what I was producing sounded sort of like music. And it felt good to make it. If Abuelo hadn't been so intent on cheating my way to the top, he might have noticed that I was getting better.

Abuelo stalked around the room, glaring at all three of us. Around ten seconds in, he slapped at the sheets on DeSean's music stand, like he was trying to scatter them. Nothing actually happened, just like when he tried to catch the glass musical note I'd dropped, but I didn't like what he was trying to do.

Making eye contact with Abuelo, I blew one wrong note on purpose.

Abuelo raised his hands and backed away. Message received.

"That was better," Mr. Edwards said, "apart from that one note, Benny."

I nodded. "Yeah, don't know what happened there. I'll keep working on it." Hopefully, Abuelo caught the *working* part. If I made this quartet, it was going to be because I was actually good enough. I would not let Abuelo sabotage my friend.

"Hey, DeSean," I said, suddenly inspired, or maybe just wanting to drive my point home, "here's something I learned from my grandfather. You keep putting your pinkie finger in the hook on top. If you keep it out of there, your third valve finger has freer movement."

Abuelo clenched his fists and practically *vibrated* with anger for a moment, and then disappeared in a huff.

Well, too bad for him. He wanted to move on to that great party in the sky, but I was going to be left behind when he did. I wasn't going to chase away any friendships.

♫ ♪ ♩ ♩

LATER ON, AT lunch, several band kids waved when I got to the cafeteria. Aaron called out, "Hey, Maravilloso! There's room over here!"

I walked over and fist-bumped Aaron and some other

band members. "Thanks, guys, but I've got a project I'm working on today. Catch you later?"

The guys gave me a hard time for not sitting with them, but they were smiling as they did it. I was starting to think of a few of them as real friends—especially DeSean. I hadn't seen Andrea in a couple of days, though. She'd texted me that she'd been researching possible reasons Abuelo was still around and had discovered interesting results.

I found her at our usual table. She had on a black T-shirt with a manga character I didn't recognize, and underneath that a long-sleeve one with white and black stripes. I could swear that the dress on the manga character was identical to one I'd seen Andrea wear.

I joined her and took out the lunch Abuela packed for me. As soon as I unwrapped the sandwich, my mouth watered from the smell of pork and mojo. And the tostones on the side would keep me full for the rest of the afternoon.

I took a bite of the sandwich and my eyes widened with pleasure. Abuela's pan con lechón had a subtle extra *tang* that nobody else's had—how did she do it? I'd have to ask her in our next cooking lesson.

Andrea slid her tablet across the table. "I've been researching your grandfather, trying to figure out what his unfinished business could be. I found a *lot*. Most people have a small internet footprint, but your grandfather had a whole shoe store."

In the empty seat next to me, Abuelo preened. "Yes, well, I was a star," he agreed.

I looked at the screen. "What did you find?"

"Well, his band was originally led by one of the other members, but Ignacio took over when the media focused more attention on his own playing."

Abuelo waved a hand dismissively. "As she said, I was the draw. Nothing wrong with that." He must have seen something in my face, because he went on, "I'm sure the others in the band were upset, but the label, the media, everybody wanted more of me. What was I supposed to do?"

I glanced at him, then back to Andrea. "Well, clearly he was the most talented. That's why all the attention was on him. He probably *should* have been leading."

"I guess. But then Ignacio left the band to go solo, and when he did, the former leader refused to resume his position. He was too hurt about being replaced. So they didn't have a leader anymore at all."

Abuelo shrugged. "They didn't need me."

"Did they need him?" I asked.

"Well, they broke up when they didn't find a new bandleader."

"These were professionals, mi nieto. This was not a social club. When one gig dries up, you find a new one."

I swallowed another bite and said, "Well, it's business, right? Was it my grandfather's fault they couldn't replace him?"

Andrea frowned. "Maybe not. But the fact remains that the band fell apart after he left, and he never looked back." She touched the screen, switching from one tab to another. "I also read that he made his personal staff go on tour with him all over the world to carry out their jobs."

Abuelo waved a hand across the table. "They *wanted* to do that! What could be better than going on tour with a star musician?"

I glanced at him and back to Andrea. "Honestly, traveling around with a concert tour sounds like a lot of fun. I mean . . . doesn't it?"

"Yeah, but not if it means missing out on holidays and events with their own families. He made one of them miss their daughter's wedding!"

I shot Abuelo a look, and he winced guiltily and looked away.

"Oh. I guess that is pretty bad," I admitted.

Andrea stole one of my tostones, and I let her because at least she had enough sense to stay away from the pork. "Just so you know, I was right about his house being historic. It was some oil guy's winter home in the 1920s, and then it became a museum, and when it was open to the public, they used to hold community events there, like Easter egg hunts, outdoor concerts on the lawn, farmers markets, stuff like that. In fact, your grandfather played one of those concerts before his band got signed to a major label."

"Okay, so?"

Andrea took a sip of fruit punch. *"So,"* she said, after swallowing, "when he bought the place, he ended all that."

Abuelo rested an elbow on the table and sighed. "Well, yes, that's true . . . but I, ah, had to protect myself. From fans. You don't know this, but sometimes people are crazy! Dangerous, even!"

It sounded reasonable, but something in the way he said it felt phony. Couldn't he have hired security? Or just stayed somewhere else during the events? He always claimed to have a good reason, but he always somehow ended up doing whatever he wanted. My eyes narrowed as I thought about how he wanted to sabotage DeSean back in our practice session. I bet if he could have done it, he would have given me a justification for it later.

Andrea seemed to think my suspicion was for her, because she held out a hand and said, "The point is not that he was bad, B. It's that there are a lot of people who believe that he wronged them, whether he did or not. Any one of them could be the cause for him still being here."

Abuelo slapped the table soundlessly. "I've heard enough. We already *know* why I'm here—to make you a star! And it's *working*! You are getting better and better even when I don't help you! Why is she digging into my past, and why are you encouraging her?"

I glanced at Abuelo, then back at Andrea.

"Why do you keep looking to your left?" she asked.

"He says you're wrong about a lot of this."

Andrea's eyes widened. "Wait—he's *here*? Right now?"

She reached across the table to feel for his presence or cold spots or whatever. This time she had the right general area.

Abuelo tried to slap her away like she was an annoying bug, but his hand passed right through hers.

"That's so amazing!" Andrea said. "We can ask him questions about the things I read, and maybe narrow down who he wronged the most."

Abuelo stiffened. "I will not answer questions! I will not be interrogated by this child! Why are you letting her—" He sputtered incoherently, then disappeared like he did every time he played the trumpet through me. The next thing I knew, I felt a familiar feverish tingle and tightness in my skin.

Before I could even think, I was picking up one of Abuela's tostones and trying to throw it at Andrea. He had taken over again! What was he thinking? I'd only given him permission to do this at home, and only when we were playing the trumpet. He had no right to use me this way!

My aim wasn't very good, though—or rather, *Abuelo's* aim wasn't very good—because we missed by a mile. The plantain chip bounced off the back of some kid's head at the next table, and then disappeared on the floor somewhere.

Suddenly back in control of my own body, I froze and tried to seem extremely interested in my food. The kid didn't look at me. He must not have seen what hit him, because I was probably the only one around with tostones in front of me.

The kid spied somebody he knew and bellowed, "Sammy, was that you?" He picked up a Tater Tot covered in ketchup and nailed his target on the forehead.

Not willing to let it end there, Sammy grabbed a half-full container of apple juice, and that was the point where I lost track, because suddenly a whole food fight was on.

"What is *wrong* with you?" I hissed at Abuelo.

"What did I do?" Andrea objected, lifting her backpack at just the right time to block a barrage of flying raisins. They bounced away harmlessly.

"Not you," I said, then jabbed my thumb toward Abuelo. "You Know Who. I can't believe he started this."

Andrea leaned in and cupped her right hand to the left of her mouth and whispered, "Pretty sure you did."

"Well, technically, yes. But I didn't mean to. I—"

"It's okay," Abuelo cut in. "Nobody saw where the tostón came from."

"*I don't care about the stupid tostón!*" I snapped. "I care that you made me throw it." I held up my arms and shook them in his face. "In case you forgot, these are mine, not yours!"

"Incoming!" someone shouted, and I looked up just in time to see a mustard-covered hot dog sailing toward us like a missile.

"Duck!" I yelled to Andrea. We both slid under the

table, the hot dog narrowly missing us and hitting the floor with a splat.

She crouched beside me with a huge smile on her face. "I've never seen a real food fight! This is like my play come to life! That's why you started it, huh? So I could see if I got the details right?"

No. But her explanation beat the real reason, that my abuelo had taken over my body without my permission, and that the tostón had been meant for her.

"Um, maybe . . ." I gave her a half shrug.

"Thought so," she said with a smile. "We can talk more about your grandfather later. Right now, I need to pay attention!" She stuck her head back out to watch and immediately got hit by flying spaghetti, but she didn't seem to mind. She actually laughed. She turned back toward me and grinned as she picked a wayward strand of spaghetti out of her hair. "No way am I missing this. I'm about to do some rewrites!" With that, she climbed out over the bench, tucked her tablet under her arm, and joined the fray.

Meanwhile, Abuelo crouched next to me under the table, viewing the chaos with a bored expression. "Kids . . . no self-control."

That was all it took to finally set me off. "What's gotten into you?" I shouted.

He turned toward me, his eyes wide with shock. "What's gotten into me? What's gotten into *you*! That is not how you speak to your elders. Especially not the great Ig—"

I clenched my fists. "Abuelo, you took over when I didn't say you could!" I interrupted.

"You didn't seem to mind when I helped out for your band audition."

"That was different," I said, biting my lip. "You thought that would be enough to get you into the afterlife party. And I believed you were really trying to help me—even when I didn't want you to. But this was not a band audition. This had nothing to do with making me a star. You tried to make me attack Andrea! Well, throw a tostón at her. But still, not cool."

"Ah, lighten up, mi nieto. She's fine. Look, she's laughing."

"Well, I'm not!" I crawled out from under the table and stood up. He materialized beside me, watching the French fries and apple slices fly with a hint of amusement in his eyes. "This isn't funny. None of this is funny! You need to go."

"But, mi nieto—"

"Get out, get out, get out!" I cried.

Abuelo opened his mouth, but it was Andrea's voice I heard. I spun to find her standing close by, her tablet still tucked under one arm and a lunch tray poised at an angle over her head. She had clearly been using it as a shield, and it was splattered with a gross mix of yogurt, orange salad dressing, and a smear of what I could only hope was apple sauce.

"Fine, I will," she said, looking hurt as she lowered the tray, gathered up her things, and hurried out of the cafeteria.

"No, Andrea, wait!" I called after her. "I wasn't talking

to—" That's when a half-open ketchup packet smacked against my cheek and stuck there. I brushed it off in disgust, and by the time I looked up, Andrea was gone.

"See what you did?" I whined, whirling to face Abuelo, but he had disappeared too. Figures. As I grabbed a napkin and wiped the ketchup off my face, it suddenly hit me that if Abuelo was as great as I had believed, he wouldn't have been locked out of heaven. Why had that never occurred to me before? I thought about Guillermo rolling his eyes at the portrait of my grandfather on the stairs, and then how Andrea said Abuelo didn't let his employees have time off, not even for the holidays. Maybe Guillermo really wasn't that sad to see the last of Ignacio Ramírez.

Maybe all this time I'd been looking up to a guy who didn't deserve it.

ABUELO HAD THE good sense to stay away from me almost all the way to dismissal time. His good sense finally dried up during seventh period, when I was washing my hands in an otherwise empty boys' bathroom.

"Benny, please, let's talk," he said, startling me.

I accidentally splashed water all over myself. Glaring at his reflection in the mirror, I said, "The last thing I want to do is talk to you, and the last place I want to talk to *anybody* is here."

"This was the first place I've been able to find you alone, mi nieto."

"Don't you 'mi nieto' me. And I'm alone because it's a bathroom, and if there's one place people are supposed to leave you alone, *it's in the bathroom*!"

He held his hands out away from his body, in a calming motion. "I got carried away in the cafeteria. I know. But you have to understand—"

"Are you serious?" I turned and stared at him. "I have to understand? After what you did, you're going to try to convince me that I'm the one who needs to understand you?"

"I see you're upset right now, so—"

"Oh, you see I'm upset. Good job. I'm impressed." I leaned on the sink.

He wagged a finger at me. "Now, listen here, Benicio—"

"You took over my body, without my permission, and you tried to make me throw something at a friend. If you can't see how terrible all of that is, then you don't *deserve* to have an afterlife. So here's what *you* need to understand. I'm done letting you take over my body. *Ever.* Do it again and I'll dump your trumpet in the bay and we'll see how the audition goes then."

He sighed. "Benny, cálmate."

"Say you understand."

"What?"

"Say you understand."

He looked away, but he said, "Fine, I understand. It's better this way anyway. As you've said, it needs to be you who learns how to play."

The door swung open and a younger kid walked in. Peering at me, he asked, "Who are you talking to?"

"Just practicing my lines for drama class," I said.

"Oh, yeah," he said, nodding.

One good thing about this school, that excuse could pretty much never fail.

WHEN WE GOT home, we could barely get to the front gate, thanks to a half dozen cars parked on the grass by the street. I leaned up against the car window, and Manny and Cristina pressed against me, all of us trying to figure out why our house had become the center of a traffic jam.

Right outside the gate, we saw Abuela's truck, its window awning propped up and a line of customers standing in front.

After we parked on the street, Mami marched out to the patch of asphalt where Abuela had set up shop. She didn't bother going to the counter. Instead, she tugged on the back door of the truck. "Gloria, what are you doing?"

Abuela glanced over her shoulder and went back to ladling some congrí onto a plate next to a pan con lechón.

"Luisa, I have been stuck inside Ignacio's shrine to himself for two weeks, and I was going to start climbing the walls if I didn't get out for a while."

I inhaled, my mouth watering as I took in the garlic from her cooking. I had barely gotten to eat any of my sandwich today before it had been knocked off the table, and I desperately wanted another one.

"Is this even legal?" Mami asked.

Abuela laughed. "Who is going to shut me down when they taste *this*?" She gave her huge frying pan a shake, making it sizzle. "Anyway, eat, help, or get out of the way. I've got business to do." Spotting me, she added, "Benicio, why don't you join me? We'll make this one of your cooking lessons."

I squeezed past Mami before she could think it over. "Yes!"

I looked at the counter where Abuela prepped the food and saw that she had spread a thin layer of cream cheese on the sandwich bread. So *that* was her secret!

Mami shook her head, but she let us be and went into the house. Once she was gone, I threw myself into helping Abuela. While she went back and forth between heating some already-roasted pork in a pan, assembling sandwiches, and heating them on the sandwich press, I kept her supplied with cut Cuban bread, thinly sliced onion, and fresh mojo. It was nice to get lost in the rhythm of dicing and chopping, the steady *thunk thunk thunk* taking my mind off other stuff I didn't want to think about—like ghosts or food fights or Andrea or whether Abuelo cared about anybody but himself.

I was glad to be here, doing this with Abuela. I knew she loved all three of us grandkids, but cooking together was *our* thing.

When the orders slowed down for a bit, I almost asked Abuela about what Andrea had discovered. If anybody would know if the stories were true, it would be my grandmother. But I remembered the way that my asking about the past made her sad, the way that so many of her memories of Abuelo were not happy ones, and I didn't want to ruin this moment, so I kept my questions to myself.

Thinking about that made me realize that Abuelo had not reappeared since I'd been here with Abuela. Somehow, I hadn't noticed until now. Somehow, I hadn't missed him.

I wasn't sure how to feel about that.

CHAPTER TWELVE

I took the same book in and out of my locker three times before I caught myself. Might as well leave it, then. Before going home, I had to head to Ms. Shankar's office for our first family session, and by the time that ended I probably wouldn't want to do anything I didn't have to. I had no assignments that absolutely *had* to be done tonight anyway.

I locked up and shuffled down the hall, wishing this whole thing would go away. Mami seemed to have decided that I had been talking to an imaginary friend. I cringed at the thought of her telling Ms. Shankar that for two reasons: (1) I was way too old for an imaginary friend; and (2) I hadn't really spoken to Abuelo since the food fight a couple of days ago.

But it's not like that explanation would sound any better. *Don't worry, Mami. You won't catch me talking to myself anymore because I'm giving my dead grandfather the silent treatment!* I could just tell them about Abuelo, but I had a feeling that would make everybody a lot *more* worried about me. I wished I'd never told Mami I'd back her up on this plan.

But not only had I agreed to this session, I'd convinced Cristina and Manny just like Mami had asked. Once I'd found stories online about how each of their favorite performers had therapists, they were more than ready to participate.

I turned at the end of the hall and saw some familiar-looking kids. It took me a moment to remember that they were classmates of Manny's.

"We should do it Saturday, so we don't have to worry about school in the morning," one said.

"You wanna invite that new kid?"

They hadn't seen me yet, so I backed up behind the corner.

"You mean Manny?" one of them asked.

I crossed my fingers. *Manny!*

Yes, I thought. *Please. Invite the new kid.*

"What's the point? He doesn't even talk to anybody anymore! He just . . . grins."

A third voice chimed in. "There's staying in character and then there's just weird."

"Have you seen those doodles all over his script? I saw one where he had drawn a mallet right where his character asks Alice about playing croquet with the queen, and it wasn't half bad, actually, so I told him so, and instead of saying *thanks* or anything, he looked at me and meowed!"

I blew out a breath. Manny was funny and kind, but he was keeping that a secret from these kids. I guess this was why we needed the group sessions—nobody *else* had a ghost helping them fake it till they made it.

I turned and took a different path. When I finally got to Ms. Shankar's office, I was the last to arrive, which meant I opened the door to find everybody staring at me from around a big circular table.

"It's about time *you* showed up," Cristina muttered. Next to her, Manny glared but said nothing.

"Hi, Benny," Ms. Shankar said, leading me to a seat. "We've just been talking about the move. Your brother and sister were telling us how it's been rough for them. How has it been for you?"

What was I supposed to say—that half the band called me Maravilloso and I was finally being treated the way Cristina and Manny had all their lives? Or that I didn't deserve any of it?

I shrugged. "It's okay, I guess."

Abuelo suddenly appeared, leaning against a bookshelf. "*Okay?* Mi nieto, you are a star!" I did my best to turn away without making anybody else think I was snubbing them.

I'd never been able to hold a grudge before, but I still wasn't over the tostón he made me throw. When I'd confronted him about it, he'd explained and explained and explained, but the one thing he hadn't done at any point was *apologize*. I was still doing my part to get him to the afterlife—I wasn't so mad that I wanted to take away *eternity* from him—but I was done listening to his stories about how amazing and successful he'd always been.

It did make our rehearsal sessions a bit awkward, though.

Things were still kind of awkward between Andrea and me too. I did text her to explain that I hadn't been yelling at *her* that day in the cafeteria, but I wasn't sure she believed me.

Ms. Shankar sat on the opposite side of the table now and gave me a probing look. "Your mom said that you felt like you had to channel your grandfather. Your father says you've been practicing the trumpet every night, and even going out to the park on Saturdays and Sundays so you can play for hours without disturbing the family."

That last part hadn't exactly been my choice—Mami had said that even with the mute on Abuelo's horn, I was giving her a migraine by going on for so many hours. But I *had* been practicing a lot.

The funny thing is, it had been torture at first, and I'd only done it because I got roped into it, and then to try to help Abuelo, but the more I played by myself, the better I got and the more I actually liked it.

"He's picked it up amazingly fast!" Papi chimed in. I blinked. That really brought home how much more time Papi was spending with us since the move—back in L.A., he seemed to work day and night. He wouldn't have known if I was learning the trumpet or the kazoo.

"That's wonderful, but . . ." Ms. Shankar rubbed her chin. "This need to be a good musician—this is new, isn't it?"

"I guess?"

"Your grandfather was a musician. Do you find yourself thinking about him a lot?"

My throat dried up. What had Mami said to her? Did she tell her about my so-called imaginary friend? I wondered if Mami had heard some of my other conversations with Abuelo and figured out who I was talking to.

I sat up. I needed to give her what she wanted to hear in a way she would believe. "I . . . well, I live in his old house, surrounded by his stuff, and I go to an art school where everybody knows about him. Maybe that's what made me try to learn to play the trumpet. I felt worried about fitting in." Gesturing around the table, I tried to change the topic. "But I'm doing fine. I don't miss L.A. much. I mostly just worry about everybody else. I know how hard Manny and Cristina and my mom and dad work, and I can see how stressed out or sad they are, and it makes me sad too. I wish I could do something to help fix things."

I may have been trying to tell her what she wanted to

hear, but when I was done, I realized everything I'd said had been true. Maybe I was more stressed than I knew.

Papi squeezed my shoulder. "You've always been so loving of everybody else, but you don't have to carry all that."

"I see," Ms. Shankar said. "You haven't mentioned whether you are *enjoying* playing the trumpet. If you are, that's great, but if not..."

"I am," I rushed to reply. "Enjoying it, I mean." I'd worked hard for my place in the band. I wasn't about to give it up now.

She shifted a bit in her chair. "What about you, Cristina? Your mom says you've been unhappy in the dance program. Is that true?"

Cristina's face fell. "Kind of. I may not be as good a dancer as I thought. I'm *definitely* worse than Sarah," she said with a mild sneer. "I've been trying to stick it out, but I can't even get my dancing-mouse part right."

"So? Like most of our students, you strike me as somebody who needs to express herself. You've got options here—why not take advantage of them? It's okay to explore."

"Don't listen to her," Abuelo said. "If you want to get anywhere, you need to stick to what you are good at!"

Cristina tilted her head. "Okay. I'll check out the course list again and let you know."

"Nonsense!" said Abuelo. "You are a Ramírez! We are not quitters!" He tried to nudge me. "Tell her!"

I took a breath to say something but stopped myself. I was through being a mouthpiece for Abuelo. This was about Cristina and what she wanted. But I really couldn't imagine her not dancing. I remembered once, when I was eight, I got up early and headed to the living room to play video games, but Cristina was already there, listening to music and dancing around in her pajamas with a big smile on her face. She didn't dance because she got applause for it; she danced because dancing was her life.

Cristina leaned against her armrest. "It doesn't change things, though. Even if I try a new art, it won't change the fact that I miss my friends and I miss our old school."

"Yeah," Manny chimed in. "And I miss our old house. Our new house is so big, I never see anyone. And I feel like I need an Uber just to get to the bathroom." He swallowed. "I miss a lot of things," he added, barely audible.

His eyes met mine, and I glanced away. He didn't come right out and say he missed sharing a room with me, but he didn't have to.

Cristina crossed her arms. "Why did we have to move here? We could have sold Abuelo's house and stayed in L.A."

Abuelo waved a hand dismissively. "¿Los Ángeles? Where they have earthquakes and drought and no Cuban food? You should be grateful to be here!"

Papi rested his elbow on his knee. "I miss some things about our old life too, but it wasn't perfect."

"You were a producer!" Manny said. "You worked on TV shows! Why would you want to live anywhere but L.A.?"

Papi sighed. "So, here's the thing," he began.

Cristina and I shared a look. Were we about to get the details on why Papi had been fired?

"I was pretty successful, yeah," he said. "But I was working six, seven days a week in the office and then going around town taking meetings, trying to pitch my other projects. And half of them didn't even go anywhere."

"Is that why you got . . . fired?" I asked hesitantly.

Papi gave me a puzzled look. "Fired? I wasn't fired. What made you think that?"

I glanced at Cristina for support, but she seemed suddenly fascinated by her cuticles. In other words, I was on my own.

I shrugged. "I don't know. I just figured we wouldn't have been so quick to up and move to Miami unless we had to."

Papi shook his head. "Well, we *did* have to, but not for the reason you thought." He sighed. He paused for a moment as Mami reached over and took his hand, and then continued, "I quit because my health was starting to suffer—I wasn't getting enough sleep, wasn't getting any exercise. And the worst part—I wasn't spending any time at home with all of you."

"Why didn't you tell us that before?" Cristina asked,

finally drawing her attention away from her nails and meeting Papi's gaze.

He squeezed Mami's hand. "I was trying to avoid worrying you kids. I had begun to remind myself of Ignacio, and that was the last thing I wanted. But I wasn't sure what to do about it—not until I got word that we'd inherited his house."

Abuelo took a step back like he had been punched.

"What do you mean, that was the last thing you wanted?" I asked.

Papi turned in his chair, his eyebrows raised. "Your grandfather was an amazing musician. But as a father? Well, not so amazing. I wouldn't have minded if he'd been less talented or successful, if he would have been around more."

Abuelo leaned over my chair. "You tell him this, Benny. Repeat what I say, word for word. Ignacio Ramírez's tours and appearances paid for your schooling, for your summer drama camp, for your braces. You name it, Ignacio Ramírez paid for it. You should be more grateful."

I fought the urge to shoo him away. I was still mad at him, and the last thing I wanted to do was let him speak through me. But at the same time, I had to know if what he'd said was true. If I couldn't get the full story out of Abuelo, maybe I could get it from Papi. After a moment, I cleared my throat and asked, "But didn't Abuelo pay for your schooling and summer drama camp and your braces?

He wouldn't have been able to do all that without going on tours and making appearances, right?" When I finished, everybody in the room stared at me.

Papi cocked his head. "How did you know about drama camp and braces?"

"You . . . mentioned it at some point." I swallowed. "I mean, obviously, since I know, right?"

"Right . . . ," Papi said slowly. "Yeah, Ignacio's work paid for all that, but it would have meant more to have him show up at any of my plays. To have him say he was proud of me. Just like I'm proud of how quickly you've learned the trumpet, and all the time you've been putting in, practicing every night, basically teaching yourself to play. It's amazing. I'm in awe of you, Benny."

Everybody else nodded and murmured in agreement.

"Yeah, bro, I threw you under the bus when I said you could play the trumpet, but then you went and learned how," Manny said. "It's amazing."

My mouth went dry. They didn't know about my secret supernatural advantage.

I couldn't help wondering how much I might have learned if Abuelo had been teaching me all along, when he was alive. "If you wanted Abuelo more involved in our lives, why didn't you ever invite him to visit us?"

Papi ran a hand through his hair. "Ah, well . . . actually I did. Many times. To your birthday and your fifth-grade graduation. To Cristina's recitals, and to Manny's plays. He was always too busy. There was always another show, another event, another commercial. Eventually, I gave up."

I turned to Abuelo. He rubbed his forehead but didn't contradict Papi.

Because it was true. Papi hadn't kept Abuelo away from my fifth-grade graduation. *Abuelo* had kept Abuelo away.

"Well," said Ms. Shankar, bringing her hands together. "Everybody has some homework. Cristina, you need to think about if there's something else you want to explore artwise. But the rest of you can be similarly thinking about things you can try out in this new life, in this new town. You won't stop missing your old lives if all you do is look backward. You need to try different things. Make memories here. So I want you to come up with a six-month plan of ways you will explore Miami. And then I want you to do as many of those things as you possibly can, but *together*, as a family."

ON THE RIDE home, everybody else talked about their "homework," so they didn't really notice that I didn't join in. Instead, I stared out the window, watching the trees go by. I felt like I had been smacked in the head by what I'd learned from Papi, but I wasn't sure why. I mean, I knew, didn't I? I had seen Abuelo be selfish, petty, full of himself. So why was I feeling like this was some new revelation?

I suppose it was because I had confirmation. Every awful thing Andrea had learned was probably true also. Abuelo was who everybody said he was.

And it hurt more, understanding how much Abuelo had hurt Papi and Abuela Gloria, because they both deserved better. Look at how much Papi had given up because he wanted to be a better father to us than Abuelo had been to him. And how Abuela had closed her restaurant for pretty much the same reason.

I excused myself as soon as we got home and went up to my room.

Of course, the moment I got there Abuelo showed up.

He reached out a hand. "Benny—"

I turned away.

Apparently, taking hints was not one of his many gifts. "Benny, mi nieto, let me explain."

I flipped open the clasps on the trumpet case. "You have an explanation for why you lied and let me believe that Papi kept you from going to my graduation? Or is it an explanation for why, even when you were in town, you couldn't make time to see your grandkids? You don't care if I blame Papi for the things you didn't do, or if Andrea blames me for the things you *did*." I pulled the trumpet out. "I was so excited when I first realized who you were. My grandfather the star. I thought you were such a good man. But now I think . . . now I'm not sure."

"At least listen to my side of things."

He started going into some kind of justification for being the worst, but I didn't hear it, because I put the horn up to my lips and blew a loud C every time he spoke. Finally, his shoulders slumped, and he closed his mouth.

"I need to practice," I said. "You know, so you can do what you did the whole time you were alive. Go to your party, have fun, and never see your family again."

CHAPTER THIRTEEN

I took to bringing Iggy with me when I practiced in the park. The spot I had found was just a few minutes away, and I liked to think it made Iggy happy to have a change of scenery. He had been eating better since we started buying higher-quality dog food. Now and then it came with a dribble of whatever tasty sauce Abuela and I had cooked up that day, and since I was the one who did the dribbling, he liked to follow me everywhere.

He didn't run around—maybe he was too old for that. He just sat beside me on my favorite bench, one that peeked out between the mangroves and gave a relaxing view of the bay, wagging his tail while I tried to make music. Unlike Mami, Iggy did not get migraines.

Win-win-win.

Abuelo and I still worked together in my room sometimes, but it was just me playing and him listening and giving feedback, like a private tutor. And then I'd go out and practice on my own, the same as any other kid. I'd told Abuelo that if he took over my body one more time, I'd refuse to do anything else for him. So he'd just have to possess me all the way up to the audition. After what I had learned last week in Ms. Shankar's office, I was only one more selfish act away from letting him worry about his own afterlife.

At least Abuelo had respected my request that he back off and give me some space. I think he had been a bit surprised to learn how much he'd hurt Papi.

I was in the middle of an exercise from an old trumpet book I had found in the house—"a classic," Abuelo had called it—when my phone buzzed with a text message. I pulled the trumpet away from my mouth and made weird faces until my lips no longer felt like I'd been kissing a garden hose. About twenty feet behind me, a dog barked—or maybe it had been barking the whole time and I couldn't hear it until now.

I checked my phone. The text was from Andrea. Yes! Maybe this meant she'd forgiven me—for real this time.

> **Hey b mom and i are going halloween costume shopping if u wanna come**

A follow-up text came in even as I was typing a response.

> **Whatever we get i'll write it into my next play so we can use it more than once**

I typed back:

> **Cant. Practicing for quartet audition.**

I got a video chat notification a few seconds later.

"Hi, Andrea. Sorry I can't—"

"Isn't that audition, like, a month away?"

My stomach clenched. Just a month. It might as well be tomorrow.

"Yeah," I replied. "But I told Abuelo he couldn't teach me by taking over anymore, ever since he—well, never mind when. I'm not letting him play through me even when I'm practicing alone. It's all me now. A month isn't a long time when you're trying to become the best at an instrument you only started learning a few weeks ago."

She didn't answer right away—instead, she peered into her camera as though she had a bad signal on her end. "Okay," she finally said. "As long as that's what it really is."

"What do you mean?"

She gave a little half shrug and looked off somewhere out of frame. "As long as you're not avoiding me because you're mad at me."

I blinked. "Me, mad at you? Why would I be mad at you? I thought you were mad at me about the food fight."

She bit her lip for a moment. "I was mad, but not over the food fight. That was great research! But then you yelled at me to get out, remember?"

"I was talking to Abuelo, not you."

Andrea looked thoughtful. "Oh. Okay, but when I showed you all that stuff . . . when I showed you all that stuff about your grandfather, you seemed upset, and since then we've had lunch together a few times, but half the time you sit with your band friends, and we haven't gotten together outside of school."

Oh. "It's not that, I promise. It's because I'm trying to learn this instrument well enough to help Abuelo move on."

"Okay, phew," she said. She literally said the word *phew*, like she was reading a script. "Anyway, I was probably wrong about him. You know how the tabloids love to make up stuff about celebrities."

A bitter taste came up in my mouth. "No, I think you were right. I learned some things from my dad in the family sessions we've been having and . . . well, my grandfather was kind of a jerk. Still kind of is."

She nodded. "Well, don't judge him too harshly. People make mistakes—even the great Ignacio Ramírez—but they can grow too."

"Even ghosts?"

"Let's hope so," she said, "or why bother sticking around?"

We said our goodbyes and I dropped the phone back

into Abuelo's gig bag, gave Iggy a treat and a scratch behind his ears, and returned to my practice.

When Abuelo took over for me the very first time, I experienced something I never knew existed. The way music *felt* when you had the skill to perform it right, when you weren't fighting against your own body to put your fingers in the right place or to blow air properly, when you weren't cringing at awkward sounds. It was magical. It was effortless. Abuelo had given me a gift, because most people had to practice for hundreds of hours—thousands, even—before they tasted that. But Abuelo had also given me a curse because I *wanted* to reproduce that, but on my own, and I just wasn't there. Yet.

There were moments, though. A minute here and there where I caught the groove, where I felt the music course through me, and it was magic again. Sitting out here, running through my *Clarke Studies* with the mid-October breeze blowing in off the water and Iggy barking at squirrels in the distance behind me, I caught that feeling again and did my best to hold on to it and let it wrap around me.

I wasn't sure how long I played. I didn't want to do anything that would take me out of the zone, not even stop to check the time. It was just me, Abuelo's trumpet, and the music until my stomach started rumbling and reminded me that I hadn't eaten since breakfast. When I couldn't ignore my hunger anymore, I packed up the trumpet, threw the gig bag over my shoulder, and glanced down at Iggy. "Ready to go home, boy?"

When Iggy didn't move a muscle, I dug a treat out of my pocket and held it just out of his reach. "How about now?" He got to his paws in an instant, snapped up the treat, and wagged his tail. "You're shameless," I said with a laugh. Iggy trotted by my side all the way back to the house.

Abuela met me in the foyer when I arrived, a pinched expression on her face. "Benicio! Did you forget? I must have called you a dozen times!"

I patted my pocket and realized only then that my phone was buried in the bag and set to vibrate.

"What did I forget?"

"You were going to help me make arroz con pollo, and we said we'd take the truck out to South Beach!"

In a rush, our plans came flooding back to me. I had agreed back on Tuesday that Saturday would be the perfect day to make the meal, since it has to simmer for hours.

"I'm sorry, Abuela. I've been so focused on the audition next month."

"Now, where have I heard that before?" she murmured.

My face heated up as I realized what she meant. I'd been so mad at Abuelo for his selfishness, and now here I was being just as bad.

She must have seen something in my face, because she pulled me in for a hug. "Ay, mi cielo, I want you to go after your dreams. Whether that's music or cooking or just being happy in your everyday life. And I wanted the same for Ignacio." She drew back so she could meet my eyes. "Just not at the expense of family."

I thought about how absent Abuelo had been when he was alive. "Is that why you ended up divorcing?"

Abuela smiled sadly. "My goodness, staying in Ignacio's house seems to make us talk about him more than we ever used to."

"Why didn't you want to talk about him before?"

She sighed. "I never wanted you kids to think badly of him. Deep down he was a good man—he just got swept up when his dreams took off." She sniffed. "It would have been one thing, I suppose, if it made him happier to leave us behind, but I don't think it did. I think he just didn't notice, until it was too late." She met my gaze. "Benny, don't make the same mistakes. Don't lose sight of what's important."

"I won't, Abuela," I said, giving her a hug.

As I left her and headed up to my room, I caught a glimpse of Abuelo in the living room, just watching Abuela. For once, he didn't seem ready to go on a rant about how she had ruined his life. Instead, he looked sad. I thought he would join me upstairs, but he didn't even react as I went past.

Before I reached my door, I heard a crash from the old

media room, which we had turned into an arts room for the three of us.

Cristina's voice cried out in a frustrated, wordless shout. Something else crashed, and I heard Manny yowl.

I hurried to the door to see if something had fallen over onto them, and saw Cristina standing over her easel, which had toppled to the ground.

"Are you okay?"

She balled her fists. "No! I hate painting!"

Oh.

That's when I noticed that only the easel was on the floor. The canvas board she had been working on stuck awkwardly out of the wastebasket by the closet, next to a paint-covered paper plate. I carefully turned the board to examine it, wondering how bad it could possibly be.

It was incredible. A girl in a black tutu twirled en pointe across from a boy in dark blue. Behind them, reeds and flowers obscured the surface of a blue pond. It wasn't fair that Cristina could abandon her lifelong art and be instantly this talented at something else.

"Cristina, this is amazing! Why would you throw it away?"

Manny slinked over to my side, examining the painting wordlessly.

"Look at it," Cristina said. "Don't you see? They're ballet dancers! Ms. Vila said you should paint what's in your heart, and what's in mine is *Swan Lake* and *La Sylphide* and *The Sleeping Beauty.* Painting was supposed to take my mind off dancing, but *it isn't working!*"

I frowned. "Couldn't you decide to paint something else? A bowl of fruit, maybe?"

She shook her head. "This is all I'm inspired to do! If I don't paint dancers, I just stare at the blank canvas." She crossed her arms. "I need to switch arts. Maybe I'll try acting!"

Manny straightened hastily. "No! I mean . . . *hisssss!*"

"Well, I'm not doing *this* anymore!" With that, she stomped from the room.

I followed her into the hall. "Wait!"

At her door, she turned and put a hand up. "Sorry, Benny, but I want to be alone right now."

She closed the door, and I stood there, wondering if being there for my family meant insisting that Cristina confide in me, or giving her space.

"Mrow?" I turned to see Manny standing in the doorway to the arts room, a stuffed mouse in his mouth.

"Hey, uh, Cheshy," I said. "Any ideas how to get through to her?"

Manny shook his head slowly, took the mouse out of his mouth, and said, " 'If you don't know where you are going, any road can take you there.' "

It was another *Alice in Wonderland* quote. Too bad I had no clue what it meant. "Thanks, I guess," I said, and retreated to my own room to try to figure it out.

AFTER DINNER—arroz con pollo that Abuela held back from the batch she'd made to sell, making me regret missing out all over again—I found Abuelo in my room, eyeing a framed article about the immigrant-turned-star.

Still thinking about his glory days, then.

"Trumpet practice is over for the day," I grumbled.

Abuelo lowered his head. "I'm not here to talk trumpets, mi nieto. I'm here to talk family."

I rolled my eyes. "Family? You?"

He winced. "Okay, I deserve that. I understand that you think I was a terrible father and grandfather and husband. Mostly because I *was* a terrible father and grandfather and husband. I don't expect you to forgive me. But I am starting to think maybe there's more that I need to do here than just teach you the trumpet."

"Like what?"

Abuelo glanced around, as though he could see through the walls. Which maybe he could, for all I knew. "I've come to realize that *everybody* in this house needs something, and I'm going to do what I can to help. For starters, there's something you should see."

He walked to the door, walked *through* the door, and poked his head back in. "Come on!"

I swallowed. I wouldn't mind if he never did that again.

I grabbed the doorknob before he could repeat the trick and followed him out to the loft.

Abuelo tiptoed past the arts room, which made zero sense since he was a ghost, but I was *not* one, so I made sure to walk quietly. To my surprise, Abuelo led me not downstairs, but to Manny's bedroom.

My brother's space was neater than mine, with a bookshelf full of novels and scripts, and photos all over his walls, but no clutter on the floor.

"Okay," I whispered. "What do you want me to see?"

"The photographs."

I stepped up to the wall. Manny's pictures were of us. All from before we moved here. Making faces at the camera, building forts out of bedsheets and pillows, wearing our swimsuits at the beach. Cristina was in some of them, but I was with Manny in all of them.

I sighed and turned away from the wall, taking in the rest of the room. That's when I noticed that there was a whole space along the wall that not only had no clutter, but it had no furniture either. A space set aside like it had yet to be used since we moved in over two months ago.

A space the size of a bed.

Was Manny thinking of moving his bed?

Wait. Had he been hoping *I* would eventually change my mind and move back in with him? Did he feel abandoned by me because I never did?

Oof.

Manny walked in and did a very catlike jump when he noticed me standing there. "Benny? What are you doing here?"

Too startled to think of a good lie, I tried the truth. Well, minus the ghost part. "I was just looking at the pics on your wall."

Manny glanced away. "I should probably box all that old stuff up. Stop being homesick for L.A., just like Ms. Shankar says."

I shook my head. "Don't. They're great. I'd forgotten how much fun we had back—" I caught myself before saying *back home*. "Back in California. We should add to the photos."

Manny's eyes widened. "How?"

"We should have Sleepover Saturdays," I said. "I could come here, or you could come to my room."

"Um, have you seen your room, bro?"

I smiled. "Fair. We should start tonight." I held up a finger. "But one rule: You have to be Manny. No character acting allowed on Sleepover Saturday."

"Only if you promise not to torture me with pelican calls from your trumpet."

I held out a hand. "Deal."

Manny shook my hand and said, "I'll go grab some games from the arts room!"

I changed into my pajamas. When I returned, I saw

board games, card games, and video games stacked on Manny's bed. He had queued up a couple of our favorite animes too.

"Manny, I don't think there are enough hours in the night to do all this stuff," I said.

"Whatever we don't get to, we'll save for next week."

"Okay," I agreed, laughing. "Which of these do you want to do first?"

"None."

"Huh?" I turned away from the stack, only to find him pointing a Nerf gun at me. The second our eyes met he fired, nailing me on the forehead.

"You jerk!" I cried out, running to grab the other Nerf gun that was leaning against the wall by his closet. "When did you get so sneaky!"

"Come on, bro, I've been living as a cat for the last month!"

If portraying a cat made him sneaky and agile, pretending to be a star trumpet player had done the opposite for me. He got me way more often than I did him, for the first time I could remember. Finally, he accepted my surrender and we moved on to *LEGO Marvel Super Heroes* on his Switch.

We played until late at night. Somewhere in there I realized that though I was trying to make him feel better, I was having fun too. I'd missed my brother as much as he'd missed me.

Manny yawned after our eighty-seventh game of Uno. "I'm glad you had this idea, bro." He stretched out in the empty space on the floor.

I tried and failed to keep his yawn from infecting me. "I am too," I said.

"Maybe he might have more fun at school as a boy than as a cat." I glanced up to find Abuelo standing beside the door. I tried not to act startled as I wondered how long he'd been there.

"Good thinking," I agreed.

Manny rubbed his eyes. "What's good thinking?"

"Um, Sleepover Saturday," I said. "Best idea I've had in a long time." I rolled over to face him. "You know, I've really had fun with you tonight, with you just being you. Maybe being Manny could help you have fun with the kids at school too."

He gave me a thoughtful look. "Maybe." He pulled his pillow under his head and closed his eyes. "Anyway, I think Mami was getting ready to disown me if I pushed one more thing off the kitchen counter."

I tugged the blanket up over me.

Across the room, Abuelo watched us. When he noticed me looking, he held a finger to his lips, and the next thing I knew he was gone.

I rubbed my face. He was so aggravating. With his disappearing. Wait, no . . . not that. I yawned again. I remembered that I was supposed to be annoyed at Abuelo. He'd been selfish. He had treated Papi, Abuela, me, all of us, like we didn't matter to him at all. But here I was, back together with my brother, and that wouldn't have happened without Abuelo. I knew Manny had been missing me, I guess, but if Abuelo hadn't brought me to his room and shown me the pictures on the wall and spelled it all out for me, I might have kept Manny on the back burner like a pot of slowly simmering beans. He didn't deserve that. As annoying as he could be at times, Manny was my brother, and that made him way more important than any band audition could ever be. It had just taken me a while to figure that out.

I could see now how easy it was to get caught up in your own life and neglect the people who mattered most to you. I hated to admit it, but maybe I needed to start giving Abuelo more of a break. He seemed to be getting the picture and was actually trying, at last, and that was something.

Abuelo might have waited until he was six feet under to start caring about his family, but better late than never.

CHAPTER FOURTEEN

Ms. Shankar leaned forward in her seat. "What about you, Cristina? How did you do with the homework I gave you last month?"

On my left, Cristina picked at a loose string in the cushion of her chair. "I tried other arts, like you said." She shrugged. "I tried painting, sculpting, acting. I was okay at them, I guess, but . . . I don't know."

She was a lot better than okay. Three weeks ago, she sculpted a twirling ballerina that seemed to be in motion. As far as I was concerned, it belonged in a museum, but she dumped it in the back of her closet. And the monologue she delivered last week from *Footloose* got massive applause, according to Manny.

I leaned toward her. "What don't you know? You were terrific at all those things!"

She smiled faintly. "Thanks, but . . . they don't make me feel anything. They don't *speak* to me."

Ms. Shankar jotted something down and said, "It sounds like you're having trouble letting go of your past. Maybe you should take a break from all the arts until you find what does speak to you."

Abuelo glared at her. "That isn't right at all! She needs *more* artistic expression, not less!"

I surreptitiously signaled him to hush.

"What about you, Luisa? Are you feeling less stressed about the new house? Is the unpacking wrapped up?"

Mami nodded. "We've managed to get Ignacio's stuff cleaned out and our kitchen set up, but . . . this party I volunteered to host . . . there's just so much to do." She sighed. "I have to figure out the food, the entertainment, the music. I'm pulling my hair out."

Abuelo flipped a hand dismissively. "You teach at a school full of musicians and entertainers. And the best chef in the world is staying with you in my house right now."

I sat up in my chair. That was actually a good point.

"We can do it," I said. Mami and the others stared at me, like they weren't sure what I was saying. "I mean all of us. Together. Abuela's food truck can do the catering, and Cristina and Manny and I can take care of most of the other things. We can ask our classmates to put on a show, and we can get the word out around campus."

"Oh, Benny, that's very sweet of you, but I don't think you understand what you're trying to take on."

"Actually," said Ms. Shankar, "this is good thinking. It's important to delegate responsibilities, and you just said you were trying to figure all of this out on your own."

Papi nodded. "I can coordinate between you and the kids and my mother."

"But I'm not the only one who's stressed," Mami said. "Can you really offer to do more?" She turned to me. "Benny, you've been working so hard at learning the trumpet. Do you really think you'll have time to do anything else?"

That was fair, but it reminded me too much of how when Abuelo was alive, he didn't have time for anything but his music, and how he was finally starting to see that had been a mistake. "I'll do the best I can with the music, but family comes first."

My trumpet-playing had come a long way, even since I stopped letting Abuelo play through me. I was probably not quite as good as DeSean, but nobody was laughing at me anymore when I played. And the sheet music was starting to make a little more sense, as long as it didn't have sharps or flats beside the clef.

I might still screw up in a lot of other ways—like the time I knocked over a whole row of music stands last week.

Aaron had put down his drumsticks and said it was too loud to hear himself play. But who hadn't had an accident or two? Or three?

I looked around at Papi and Cristina and Manny. They didn't have to say anything for me to know they were ready to dive in.

"We've got this, Mami."

CRISTINA PUT DOWN her marker and pushed the sheet of poster board she'd been working on into the center of the glass tabletop. "Done!"

Again.

"It's not a race," I said, mostly because, if it were a race, I'd be losing.

I turned her newest poster so I could see what she'd come up with this time. A guy and a girl were dancing, connected by one hand, one of the girl's feet high, like she was kicking up her heels. DANCE THE OLD YEAR AWAY! was written across the top in angled letters.

I laid it beside my own poster. NEW YEAR'S EVE PARTY, mine said, inside a crooked box.

Abuelo paced around the covered patio. "Ay, Benny, that poster is like my body after I had the heart attack: no life! Try the glitter."

If anybody was going to demand more glitter, it was of course going to be my grandfather. Still, he had a point. I really needed to up my game. I reached for the glue.

I got to work on embellishing my creation, only to be startled what seemed like seconds later by Cristina's next cry of "Done!"

This time her poster had a popped-out layer she'd made from construction paper glued onto the board, giving the whole thing a 3-D effect. It was Cinderella at the ball, but the text said, YOU WON'T WANT TO LEAVE BEFORE MIDNIGHT!

"Wow," I said. "These are all amaz— Wait a minute."

She tugged on one of her nails. "What? You don't like it?"

I shook my head. "I *love* it, except . . ."

"Except what?"

I pointed to each of her other posters. One featured a sock hop, and one showed an old man tap-dancing off a stage to the right while a baby in a HAPPY NEW YEAR sash hula-ed in from the left. "Have you looked at these?"

"Benny, I *made* them."

"Yeah, but have you *looked* at them?"

She glared. "What about them?"

"All your posters are about dance."

Her brow furrowed, and she focused on the posters as though seeing her work for the first time.

Abuelo turned midstride. "She is still a dancer in her heart," he said, "and that's what she should be doing."

Abuelo and I didn't always see eye to eye, but in this, he was spot on. "I think maybe, deep down inside, you can't stop thinking about dance." I glanced at the posters again. "Or not so deep down."

Her face fell. "I do miss dancing. But I can't crawl back now! It would be humiliating! So much time has passed, and everybody else has been practicing and getting better. What if I beg to play a dancing mouse, and the next role's just as bad or worse? What if I'm really just not that good?"

"That's ridiculous," I said. I had to stop myself before adding *You are a Ramírez.*

"I wasn't that good when I started," Abuelo said. "You get better when people point out to you where you are missing the mark."

I stared at him. Did Ignacio the Great just admit to being less than great? This was literally the opposite of every piece of advice he'd ever given me.

"Are you okay? Why are you staring at the screen door?"

I turned back to Cristina. "I was just thinking, that's all." After a moment, I added, "You know, Abuelo wasn't very good when he first took up the trumpet."

She leaned back in her chair. "What? That's not what I've always heard!"

"Yeah, I think people like to build up legends to sound like they were always fantastic."

Abuelo looked off into the distance. "The first time I

auditioned for the band, Señora Ruíz told me I needed more lessons before I was ready, and also that I had no sense of rhythm. Can you imagine how humiliating that was, mi nieto? For a Cuban to have no rhythm?"

I passed this along to Cristina.

She cocked her head. "What did he do?"

"Spent the next year practicing more," I relayed. "And found good teachers who helped him get better."

Abuelo gestured with his hand a couple of times, like he was trying to force something out that he was reluctant to admit. "A good artist needs to be humble and able to take constructive criticism," he said finally.

I stared at him. I wanted to ask when that stopped being true for him, but I couldn't think of a way to do it in front of Cristina. Also, that felt a little like kicking him when he was trying to do better. I supposed at some point he got so used to being praised all the time for being great that he lost sight of the humility it took to get him there, the humility he said we all needed.

"How do you know all this?" Cristina asked.

"Ah . . . I read it." I straightened the poster board in front of me. "You know all those old scrapbooks we found? There were clippings from an old magazine interview in one of them."

She nodded, but slowly. "I can't believe you read all those. I have to be honest, it's weird how you've gotten all into him since we moved here."

I shrugged. "I guess I wish I'd known him better when he was alive." I looked up at Abuelo. "Especially the version of him who wasn't a star. Sometimes you don't appreciate something until it's gone."

Cristina rubbed a stain on her jeans. "I feel like that about dancing."

"Dancing isn't necessarily *gone*, though."

"Unlike Abuelo. Good point." She sighed. "I just don't know if I can deal with how embarrassing it's going to be to ask them to let me be a dancing mouse."

"Hey. I wore a purple shirt with sequins on the second day of school. You'll live."

She snorted. "Okay, fair. You know what? I'm gonna go tell Mami I want to switch back into dance." She got up, leaned over, and kissed my cheek. "Thanks for helping me figure that out!"

I watched her run inside. I was happy at the thought of Cristina dancing again. It was what she loved best, and she had genuine talent. Between her dancing and Manny starting to be less furball and more goofball, the two of them were getting back to the brother and sister I'd been missing.

Too bad it wasn't so simple for me. The old me couldn't play the trumpet. The old me would blow this audition in two weeks, and even though I no longer *really* believed that alone would cost Abuelo his shot at the afterlife, I couldn't be sure. He needed to become a better person—that was the main thing. But what if there was some kind of point system? What if Abuelo was almost there, and me getting into the quartet, proving that he had spent quality time with at least one of his grandkids, earned him the last few points he needed to get his wings? Unlikely as that seemed, if there was even the tiniest chance of it being true, I couldn't just go back to being the old me.

Maybe instead I could find a way to be a new and improved Benny. Still myself, but just a little closer to stardom.

CHAPTER FIFTEEN

"Benny! Are you coming or not?"

I flinched at Papi's voice echoing through the house. One thing about that entry foyer: it amplified sound so much, it was like a natural intercom. I could hear him from my room as if he were standing right outside the door.

"I thought you had to be there by noon!" he added.

"Where is he?" I murmured. "Why can't I find him?" I opened my closet door, searched under my bed, even peeked out onto the balcony.

"Abuelo, where are you? I changed my mind! I'm not ready!"

I had been so sure that the only way succeeding at playing the trumpet would mean anything was if it was really me. But this morning when I woke up, panic set in as I realized that I was just not good enough to get the place in the quartet on my own. Abuelo playing through me was the only chance I had. For all I knew, it was the only chance he had too.

I peered out the window, as if I might see Abuelo on the lawn without me. I'd taken everybody's advice and tried to make sure I didn't get so focused on the trumpet that I pushed away my friends and family. I'd helped Andrea with her play, which Manny and his friends were going to perform at our New Year's party. I'd attended Cristina's dress rehearsal and watched her be the best dancing mouse anybody had ever seen. I'd had my cooking lessons with Abuela, shopped for party supplies with my parents, and hung out with Manny. But now it was time to audition, and . . . I was no Ignacio Ramírez.

"I don't want to let you down!" I said. "I give you permission! You can play!"

"Who are you talking to?"

I whirled away from the glass to find Cristina in my doorway. "Nobody!"

She cocked her head.

"Don't you talk to yourself when you're stressed?" I asked.

"Benny!" Papi shouted.

"What are you trying to find? Maybe I can help you."

"I'm . . ." What could I tell her? "I'm looking for my rock."

Her mouth fell open. "What?"

Rock? That's what I came up with? Looking for *my rock*?

"Um, my lucky rock. I've been keeping it in my pocket, and I've done really well with it, so you see? It's lucky! But you wouldn't recognize it, so you can't help me, but thank you anyway!" I smiled weakly.

"You don't need it, Benny! You'll do great!"

"Uh, sure, thanks."

"Anytime. But you *do* need that," she added, pointing to Abuelo's trumpet on its stand beside the bed.

Gah! I dragged the gig bag off its hook by the door and picked up the horn. Suddenly it felt like an alien device. I couldn't remember how to hold it. Why had my hands forgotten? For weeks this had been second nature, but now my mind was blank—was it right before left? Left before right? I didn't *know* anymore!

I put the horn away, hoping my hands would straighten themselves out on the drive, and stuffed the music I'd been planning on playing in the bag as well . . . only, one glance at the sheets told me my brain had forgotten this too. They were just hieroglyphs.

Had Abuelo given up on me, disappeared, and taken all I'd learned with him?

"Hurry!" said Cristina.

I ran past her and down the stairs. "Just a minute!" I shouted.

I had one last chance. I checked the garage, the third of it where we still had Abuelo's remaining possessions piled up. Maybe he was here spending time with his stuff before we gave it to some museum or charity.

"I need your help, Abuelo," I murmured.

I stepped between the stacks of mementos. Lots of these were objects I'd moved here from my bedroom, but many of the items I'd never seen before. Abuelo had kept so many *things* to remind him of how successful he was that they had accumulated in every room in the house. The big ones, like statuettes or advertising cutouts, I recognized, but the little things, like yet *another* scrapbook or paperweight, were easier to miss until we cleared a space.

One scrapbook in particular had RAMÍREZ neatly handwritten in big black letters on it, which was weird, because it was different from the ones I'd already seen. The others were all bound in matching purple, with IGNACIO RAMÍREZ—COMMERCIALS or IGNACIO RAMÍREZ—INTERVIEWS or similar descriptions on laser-printed labels. This was the only handwritten one, it was in a black binder, and it didn't say which part of my grandfather's stardom it chronicled. Maybe it was a gift from a fan, or maybe it was older than the others. If so, it was unlikely anybody would want it—the other ones might at least be interesting to a museum or one of those restaurants that collected memorabilia.

On top of the black scrapbook, I saw a flash drive labeled with a bit of masking tape, on which Abuelo or somebody had scrawled the words IR NEW SONG DEMOS (JUNE) in black ink. I pocketed the flash drive—this should definitely not go to a random collector. Not without me checking it out first.

"Benicio Ignacio Ramírez," Papi bellowed, "you are going to be late!"

I let out a long breath. For whatever reason, I was on my own today. Just like I'd said I wanted it.

I went out to the front step and followed Papi to the SUV.

The drive went too quickly. Papi talked the whole way. He probably said encouraging things, but I couldn't focus on his words. He didn't understand what was on the line. He didn't know I had to be perfect or Abuelo might lose his afterlife. I shoved my hands in my pockets to stop them from shaking, but that didn't keep my stomach from churning. *Get it together!* I chided myself. *Something huge is on the line and the odds are stacked against you, but you won't have a shot at all if you puke on Mr. Edwards.*

I tried my best to slow my breathing and remember what Andrea had told me about stage fright—that nerves were really just excitement, and once actors get their first line out, they're usually fine. I hoped the same would be true for me. If I could get through the first measure, maybe everything after that would be smooth sailing.

At the school, which was eerily quiet on a Saturday afternoon, I ran to the theater—SMPAS teachers and students got very touchy if you called it an *auditorium*. I was several minutes late, but Mr. Edwards greeted me as though he hadn't noticed.

Unfortunately, he wasn't judging this by himself. There were three other teachers I didn't know, holding clipboards and looking at us like we were each personally responsible for them being at school on Saturday, and so we'd better not be wasting their time.

I gulped.

I saw Harold and DeSean sitting a few rows apart. Harold didn't look up—he was too busy making notes on his sheet music—but DeSean waved me over. I smiled despite my nerves and joined him in the front row, collapsing into the seat beside him.

He nudged me with his elbow. "Good luck, Benny. Just relax and have fun!"

From anybody else, it would have just been one of those things people say because you're supposed to. But this was how DeSean really approached music. He played because he enjoyed it, and if he didn't get this part, he would keep on playing and keep on loving the art. And I knew from experience that when I played music with DeSean, it was fun for me too.

I felt the tension slide right out of my muscles. There was nothing I could do about Abuelo not being here, so I might as well do as DeSean said.

The trombone players went first, and I tried to listen to

them and forget this was an audition. Then it was time for DeSean, Harold, and me to perform.

Harold went first. He hadn't been at any of our practice sessions, since he didn't really need them. He was first chair for a reason. But as I listened to him dive into the second suite of Handel's *Water Music*, I knew why the judges didn't seem that impressed. Harold was hitting all the right notes at all the right times, but there was no soul in his playing. We might as well have been listening to a computer-generated trumpet solo. I got the feeling he became a musician because he was technically good at it, not because he liked it all that much.

DeSean was a different story. He went next, and he played the first movement of the Barat Fantasy in E-flat. His playing was beautiful, and he nailed that opening cadenza, speeding up at the end and building in volume as though his own emotions were swelling with the music. He seemed to forget where he was and what was at stake.

Whenever I played, I could pick out most of the right notes, and I tried my best to hit them all, but it took time for me to fall into a zone where I stopped worrying so much about getting every measure right and just felt the music. I bet the zone came naturally to DeSean, though. . . . I could tell he loved what he was doing. Loved the compositions, loved his instrument. He was at peace, unafraid of not being good enough, just happy making music.

I supposed it was something like that for Abuelo. For

Cristina with her dancing and for Manny with his acting. Maybe it could be like that for me someday. Sometimes I thought cooking with Abuela felt a little that way. Lately I didn't stress about how much olive oil I used or how long I had to stir the pot. I didn't always need to measure every ingredient. I could just sense when I had the right amount of chili flakes or when it was time to turn down the flame. Cooking was starting to feel as natural as breathing. I wasn't sure playing the trumpet would ever feel that way for me. But for Abuelo's sake, I hoped giving it my all would be enough.

"Okay, Benny," Mr. Edwards said, much too soon.

I stiffened, and he locked eyes with me. "Just do your best, kiddo. No pressure."

I walked to the stage with my trumpet and my music, set the sheets up on the stand, and picked up the horn, hoping for a last-minute miraculous ghostly appearance.

"Okay, Abuelo," I murmured. "Last chance."

Several seconds went past while I held the horn in front of my lips. One of the judges coughed, and somewhere in the darkness, a kid giggled.

He wasn't coming. What did that mean? Had something kept him away? Or had he come to the obvious conclusion, that I wasn't going to be good enough?

Maybe he was afraid his being here would make me nervous.

I pressed the trumpet against my lips and played.

I chose an étude from one of Abuelo's old books, which he had described as "the bible" for trumpet players, the Arban's. It was probably the easiest solo in the entire book, but it was something I felt more or less comfortable doing because I'd been practicing it on my own for weeks.

I was pretty sure it wasn't beautiful like DeSean's, or as pitch-perfect as Harold's, but it wasn't terrible. And a couple of months ago, I could do none of this. That was something. Of course, I had the best teacher anybody could imagine, using techniques nobody else could use. But right here, right now, I stood alone on the stage, and it was . . . kind of amazing. Not counting band class, I had never played for an audience before, and it surprised me to find that I liked it. It felt good to have so many eyes on me while I ran through the song, my fingers confidently pressing buttons as I blew from my diaphragm and produced music that actually sounded soothing and sweet and a little melancholy. I stole glances at the judges and DeSean. All of them were leaning forward in their seats. DeSean looked impressed, like I might be real competition. Maybe I did have a touch of that Ramírez talent running through my veins after all.

When we were done with our audition pieces, Mr. Edwards had us wait backstage.

"Great job, Benny," DeSean said. "I can tell you worked hard."

"Thanks," I said, "but your audition was killer." I glanced

to make sure Harold couldn't overhear me, and added, "I think you're gonna get it."

"No matter what happens, we should celebrate. Let's agree now, before we know: no hard feelings." He held out a fist.

"Deal," I said, bumping it with mine.

"My mom's taking me to an escape room over by Merrick Park afterward. Why don't you come? We can try to break out and then get something to eat."

I smiled. This would take the sting off whatever happened: spending time with a friend, seeing a new part of Miami, and eating some more of the city's amazing food. And I'd never tried an escape room before, though Cristina and some friends went once back in L.A. "I'm down! Let me check with my parents first, though."

Just then one of the other teachers called us back into the theater.

I zoned out while they announced the other parts—some kids jumped up and down, while others nodded and tried not to act disappointed. Finally, Mr. Edwards got to the trumpet. "The trumpet position goes to . . . DeSean Burton!" He looked at DeSean with a proud smile and added, "Congratulations, DeSean! Great work!"

Turning toward the rest of us, he added, "I'm so proud of you *all* and how hard you've worked and how far you've come." It seemed like he was looking right at me when he said that, though possibly it was in my mind.

I wasn't going to be in the quartet. But I was holding my own in band. Nobody even talked about kicking me out anymore. Just being a member of this group so soon after taking up the trumpet was pretty incredible.

But was it enough? Abuelo had helped me a lot and spent so much time trying to turn me into a star. But would his former bandmate take my not getting into the quartet as a sign that it had been too little, too late? Did this mean Abuelo wouldn't get into heaven? Why couldn't he have been here?

Something had to have shown on my face, because DeSean leaned over and murmured, "Are you disappointed?" He quirked his lip. "If you change your mind and don't want to go out, I'll understand."

I wasn't going to drag DeSean down, and I didn't want him to think I wasn't happy for him.

"Nah, man," I replied. "Let's go celebrate!"

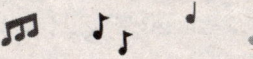

THE NICE THING about VR games was that they took all of my attention, and I could almost forget about my failed audition. It was harder at dinner to keep from thinking about Abuelo and wondering what would happen now. Would Abuelo be stuck here forever, since I didn't make the quartet?

I really really *really* wanted DeSean to believe I was happy for him, though. Because I was. It was just a challenge to keep my feelings off my face. I wished I had Manny's acting talent, but even if I slipped now and then, I hoped DeSean knew that I wanted to stay friends.

When his mom dropped me off at home, I endured a few minutes of consolation from Mami and Papi before I ran to my room so I could decompress and stop putting on a happy face. Of course, this time Abuelo was there.

"So . . . I heard the news," he said.

I shook my head. "I didn't get the part," I replied, my voice thick. "Where were you? Why didn't you come when I called? I was going to let you do it. I was going to let you take over so you could get into . . . so *I* could get into the quartet. But I couldn't find you anywhere, so I had to play on my own, and that's why I missed the notes in the tenth measure, and I wouldn't have if you had shown up and—"

"Mi nieto, I stayed away on purpose."

I blinked and backed up a step. "You did? Why?"

Abuelo gestured at the gig bag. "I wanted you to see how much you'd learned. How much better you are than you believed when you first arrived and you told me you had no talent. What you did today was *all* you."

I dropped to a seat on the edge of the bed. "But, Abuelo, I didn't get the part."

"Eh, it's fine. You did a fantastic job."

I looked up at him. "You were there?"

"Of course I was. After all the performances I missed

over the years, somebody up there gave me one more chance to make it to one. I've been a fool many times in my life, Benny, but I'm not such a fool that I would let that chance slip away."

I rubbed the side of my face. "What if I cost you the afterlife?"

Abuelo shook his head. "Don't worry about that, mi nieto. What is one more party, when I've been to so many? What I want most of all is for you to be proud of yourself. You are, aren't you?"

I thought about it for a moment. About how it felt to play and know it was me doing it. Despite myself, despite feeling bad for Abuelo, I smiled a little. "Yeah."

A knock sounded on the door, and then Papi poked his head in. "Hey, Benny . . . you came up here in a hurry." He swallowed. "I just wanted to make sure you're okay. I know you must be disappointed."

I glanced at Abuelo, who smiled. "No," I said. "I mean, I am. But I think I did all right. My friend DeSean got it, and he was terrific, and I get to stay in band and keep playing the trumpet, even if I'm not a star."

Papi stepped the rest of the way in, tousled my hair, and sat beside me on the bed. "That's wonderful, Benny. I'm so proud of you, of how hard you've worked and how much you've learned." He glanced at the gig bag. "I'm glad you found your grandfather's horn and decided to make it your own. It's got a good home with you."

I felt my face heat up, and I looked away.

"You know," Papi went on, "my father didn't talk a lot about his feelings, but I think he would be proud of you too."

"You'd better believe it, mi nieto. I'm proud of *all* of you Ramírezes, but I'm especially glad my trumpet ended up in your hands."

I couldn't help grinning at the compliment. Turning back to my father, I said, "He'd be proud of you too, Papi."

Papi glanced up at the window. "Oh, I don't know about that. I think he valued music more than anything else, and music wasn't my love like it was his. But that's okay."

Abuelo put his hands on his hips. "No," he said. "No, it is *not* okay."

I chewed my lip, wondering what he meant by that.

Ignacio pointed at the door. "Go get that scrapbook you found earlier. The special one. Show it to him."

Huh? I stared up at him.

"Go on!" he insisted. "The black one, in the garage!"

He really had been watching me the whole time I searched the house for him.

I stood. "Wait here, Papi. I have something to show you."

Did I? I was taking Abuelo's word on that. I hurried down the stairs and to the garage and grabbed the scrapbook from the pile I left it on earlier. Bringing it back, I handed it to Papi and said, "Look inside."

Papi glanced back and forth between me and the scrapbook a couple of times, and then finally cracked it open.

Inside, it was full of page after page of press clippings, but they were not about Ignacio Ramírez, star trumpet player. They were about Félix Ramírez, rising-star producer.

I skimmed the headlines:

Celia Cruz Biopic Helmed by Son of Legendary Trumpet Player.

Newcomer Ramírez Shares the Inspiration Behind Bilingual Telenovela.

Nine Biggest Surprises of the New Season: Johnson, Ramírez, Mazin, and More.

Papi put his hand to his mouth. "Where did you find this?"

"It was with Abuelo's stuff. He *was* proud of you."

He did this weird laugh, not quite a happy one. "I wish he could have told me." While Papi flipped through the pages, marveling at this bit of his own history seen through somebody else's eyes, Abuelo squatted in front of me.

"You know I've been selfish. I wasn't there when people needed me, and I didn't tell them what they meant to me. But you are absolutely mistaken if you think I didn't love Gloria and Félix. And you kids too, even if I didn't see you as much as I wish I had."

I wanted to believe him, but if that were true, he would have come to see us. Papi invited him often enough.

He seemed to read the skepticism on my face, because he sighed and said, "I know, I should have visited. I stayed away because in the handful of times I did come, seeing your father with his family reminded me of what I'd thrown away. I didn't believe he really wanted to see me. I didn't believe I would ever belong. It was easier to find excuses to stay away than to try to fix the damage I'd done. It was easier to stay busy, and to convince myself I was happier that way."

Something connected all of us Ramírezes after all—we convinced ourselves of things that weren't true. Like how Cristina believed that if she wasn't the star, she was a failure. Or how Manny believed everybody would like a pretend version of him better than the real one. Or the way I'd convinced myself I was the talentless Ramírez. Or the way Papi convinced himself that Abuelo didn't love him. How did we all get so convinced of these lies?

"I guess he didn't know how to tell people in words," I finally said. "But now you know."

Papi smiled sadly. "Now I know," he agreed. He pulled me over and kissed my head, and said, "Good night, Benny. I love you."

"I love you too," I replied, and I watched Abuelo watch his son walk out.

I should have felt happy for Papi to know a little better how Abuelo felt, but I felt sad instead that Abuelo couldn't say what he needed to say to anybody, unless it was through me. Abuelo couldn't kiss his son good night, and he couldn't hear his son say "I love you" back to him.

"He would say the same to you if he could," I said.

Abuelo just watched the door. "I hope that's true."

I straightened on the bed, suddenly sure I had figured something out. "You know, you've done so much . . . taught me to play the trumpet, helped Cristina see that she loves dancing more than she needs to be the star, helped me fix things with Manny, helped Papi see that you were proud of him, got us to help Mami with her stress. . . . Papi doesn't know all that, but if he did, he definitely would see that you've changed and that you are trying to reconnect with the family."

"You think so?" Abuelo asked hopefully.

I nodded. "That was your unfinished business. I'm sure of it. In fact, I bet you'll get to go to your party after all. Who wouldn't let you in? You may not have been great before, but you are now."

Abuelo took a deep breath. "Thank you, mi nieto." He brought his hands together. "There's still so much I haven't done, though. More I would like to teach you, if you want me to."

"Definitely!" It would be nice to learn to play better, without the pressure of Abuelo's afterlife hanging over me.

Abuelo crossed his arms and frowned. "There is one thing I need to know, however. I need for you to tell me the absolute truth."

I swallowed. "What is it?"

He backed up and spread his arms. "Why didn't you wear my lucky shirt for the audition?"

I laughed out loud and then hushed quickly, hoping nobody heard me talking to my "imaginary friend."

"It wouldn't have been fair," I said. "Harold and DeSean wouldn't have stood a chance."

"Ah, Benicio," Abuelo said. "You're right, of course!"

I chewed my lip, because at that moment, I knew I had been right about something else too. Abuelo would be moving on before long, and I would never see him again.

AFTER ABUELO HAD disappeared and I got ready for bed, I pulled out the flash drive I had found and jammed it into my laptop. I opened up the contents of the drive and set them to play, then dimmed the screen and faced it away from me so the glare wouldn't keep me up.

I should give these files to somebody, I thought. The label said it was new song demos, and somebody would definitely want that—new music from Ignacio Ramírez. But I found I wanted to hear them first. What if they weren't good? Or what if the files were corrupted?

As I lay in bed looking up at the ceiling, I realized the new music was actually *very* good. At least, *I* liked it. I recognized little flourishes and note progressions that made this music undeniably my grandfather's, but they were set in new melodies that showed he had been an artist right up until the very end.

Abuelo could be such a pain sometimes. Such a pain that it was easy to forget that he really was as gifted as he constantly claimed he was. It was nice to find a reminder of that. Of the Ramírez talent he kept insisting ran through my veins.

A thought struck me as my eyelids started to get heavy. If I really did have until New Year's Eve, then I might have an idea for a parting gift that I could give Abuelo.

CHAPTER SIXTEEN

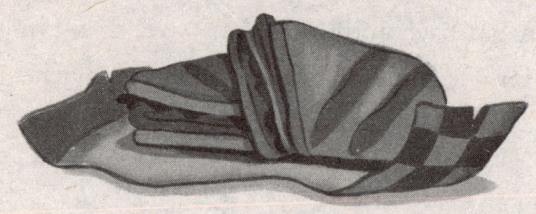

The property looked fantastic for the New Year's Eve celebration. Papi and some volunteers from school had hung colored lights from the banyan trees that bordered the yard, they'd covered the pool in silver and black balloons, and they'd hand-made giant 3-D HAPPY NEW YEAR signs out of boxes, tape, and spray paint. Mami ran from table to table, adjusting centerpieces, chatting with guests, and making sure everybody had gotten something to eat and drink.

I thought about what Andrea had told me, how this property used to host parties like this all the time. I didn't think we were up to something so huge more than once a year or so, but it sure was a sight to see right now.

Midnight was still five hours away, but here in the food truck, we were as busy as we were going to get. Andrea's mom had volunteered to help with the food, but the two of us still struggled to keep up with the line of guests. Even though Abuela had her hands full, she still found time to crack one-liners at guests who didn't choose an item fast enough.

I was making medianoche—or midnight—sandwiches, which were basically Cuban sandwiches but on sweet bread. I hadn't *purposely* set out to make a pun about midnight on New Year's Eve, but once Ms. Wade pointed it out, I played it up with every guest in line. "Get your medianoche while it's still early," I called out, "so you can celebrate midnight twice!"

With Abuela's guidance, I made them *right:* with the layer of mustard in between the Swiss cheese and the top slice of bread, so that when I pressed the sandwich on the grill, the melting cheese formed a pocket for the mustard. It slowed things down because grilling with the mustard meant I had to stop and clean the sandwich press more often, but if you waited to put mustard on until after you'd pressed the sandwich, there was no way to get it in the right layer.

For people like Cristina, who didn't like mustard at all, I made sure to grill the occasional sandwich without it. For people like Manny, who liked mayonnaise on their sandwich,

I made sure to give them directions to the fridge, where they could ruin their own meal without me or Abuela having to watch or be involved.

On the back counter of the tiny space, Abuela deep-fried empanadas. She was making two kinds today: empanadas de carne, filled with seasoned picadillo; and empanadas de guayaba y queso, which was my favorite pastry of all. The sweet guava and the tangy cream cheese, stuffed inside a warm pocket of dough so it stayed gooey and hot, were wonderful together. Abuela said I was still too young to use the deep fryer, but I kept hoping sooner or later she'd get tired of the heat and let me take over.

In the meantime, Ms. Wade made dozens of Elena Ruz sandwiches on bocadito bread. A lot of people who didn't know better gave the side-eye to the turkey, cream cheese, and strawberry jam combo, but once they tried it, they knew not to knock it.

On the other side of the counter, past the hungry crowd lining up, I caught glimpses of Abuelo wandering around, taking in the party. I couldn't quite decipher the expression on his face; it looked kind of like a smile, but a small one, not his trademark maravilloso grin. Was he happy to see a party here, or sad because he couldn't be the center of it?

I sighed. These were my last hours with my grandfather, and I was losing them. I wanted to join Abuelo and ask him directly what he was feeling, or just listen to any stories he wanted to tell me. But nobody else knew he was here, or would believe me if I told them, and I couldn't abandon my family when they needed me.

"Have you eaten anything yourself?" Andrea's mom asked.

"I had the very first medianoche I made." I patted my stomach. "You know, to test the product."

Ms. Wade nodded, her face serious but the corner of her lip rising. "Yes, of course. Well, trade with me: one of my sandwiches for one of yours. So we can be more thorough in our testing."

"For science!" I agreed, grabbing a hot sandwich off the press with a spatula and maneuvering it onto her plate.

We had gotten a bit ahead of the crowd, so I took a bite of the Elena Ruz and enjoyed the contrast between the sweetness of the strawberry jam and the slight saltiness of the turkey.

"Mmmm," Ms. Wade said. "Benny, this is better than most restaurants! You, like Gloria, are an artist!"

"A sandwich artist," I said, grinning. But... even though I knew she was playing, this really was an art, wasn't it? Abuela made creative choices, based on things she had been taught and also based on her experience, and those choices led to people enjoying what she made. How was that anything *but* an art?

It was something to think about, anyway.

I realized I'd lost track of Abuelo while I ate. I searched for him again. If I couldn't be by his side, then at least I wanted to see him as much as I could.

Tons of people milled about, enjoying the beautiful setting, and Abuela's rich food, and the performances we had lined up. The posters that Cristina and I made, along with Manny's social media push, had really turned out everybody in the SMPAS family. Even Iggy was having a good time, trotting from guest to guest and begging for handouts. I don't think too many people wanted to share Abuela's food, but Iggy got a lot of pats and scritches, and he wagged his tail constantly. It was the happiest I'd ever seen him.

Everything was going off without a hitch. Too bad I couldn't really enjoy it. Not only would I have to say goodbye to Abuelo at midnight, but Abuela would be going home soon too. I'd tried to talk her into staying, but she'd reminded me that she had a life back in Tampa she couldn't just walk away from.

A few thousand sandwiches later, it was finally time to shut the food truck down so that we could enjoy the party too. I found Abuelo and stood beside him. I couldn't talk directly to him—my family had finally stopped asking about my supposed imaginary friend, and I wasn't about to start that up again—but we could at least watch together.

The stage had been set up on the side of the yard across from the patio, so that folding chairs could be arranged on the concrete beside the pool.

Manny and some drama kids performed Andrea's one-act play about a delusional time traveler who kept going one second into the future, only nobody could tell because it took him a second to do it each time. Everybody laughed at the jokes, but nobody laughed louder than Abuelo. I watched Manny in the middle of the action, and it felt like I was seeing him for the first time. I tried to imagine how it felt for Abuelo to see his grandson perform.

The play was a hit. Andrea was determined to write spooky stories, but—whether she wanted to admit it or not—she had a talent for comedy. And Manny's facial expressions and timing were perfect for delivering her one-liners.

When the show ended, the audience broke out in applause and cheers. I joined in, determined to be loud enough for both Manny and Andrea to pick me out. After the actors took their bows, several people rushed the stage. I even saw a few ask Andrea and Manny for their autographs.

Somewhere behind me, a boy said, "That Ramírez kid is so weird, but he's really good too."

For about half a second I stiffened, until I realized that they were talking about Manny, not me.

"We're in an arts school," someone replied. "We're all a little weird. And at least he stopped acting like a cat all the time."

"Okay, true," the first kid acknowledged.

Manny was finally letting the others see him in his

comfort zone, and it made me feel like I could lift right off the ground.

Next, Cristina and some of the dancers put on a reprise of a scene from *The Nutcracker*. Again, Abuelo was transfixed. "This show about the dancing mouse, and her sidekicks the fairies and the wooden soldiers, is the best!" he said, his eyes bright.

When Cristina came off the stage, Abuelo shooed me with his hands. "Go tell her how wonderful she was!"

"Great job!" I said, as soon as she was within earshot.

"Yeah!" a voice to my right agreed. I turned to discover that it was Sarah, and stiffened, waiting for her to say something sarcastic to Cristina. Instead, I was amazed to hear "You were so into your role, and your pirouettes were flawless!"

"Thanks!" said Cristina. "But what I really wish is that I could get my arabesque as steady as yours!"

"We should get together and practice. I can show you how I do my arabesque, if you'll help me pirouette like you!"

"Deal!"

I stared at Cristina as Sarah disappeared. "I thought you said she was super mean!"

Cristina ducked her head and fiddled with the neckline of her leotard. "Actually, she isn't so bad. She's just really serious about her dancing. Once I got over my hurt feelings, I realized I could learn a lot from her."

She leaned in closer to me. "She's going to be in the

upper-grade productions next year, so if I watch and practice and get as skilled as she is, maybe I can have a shot at a lead in one of our shows once she moves on."

I blinked. "But, Cristina, didn't you hear? Mami and Papi decided to move back to California!"

She gasped. "What? We can't! Now that I've finally made friends here? How could they?"

"Kidding!" I said, a big grin on my face.

"Benny!" She shoved me lightly. "You're the worst!"

After she went off with some of her friends, Abuelo leaned in. "That wasn't very nice, mi nieto."

I glanced around to make sure everybody was paying attention to the announcer on the stage and replied, "I know, but what are little brothers for, if not torturing their big sisters? I've been taking it easy on her because she was so sad, but now I've got some catching up to do!"

Abuelo laughed and tried to tousle my hair, but of course he couldn't, which I think reminded us both that this wasn't just any old party. When this one ended, there would be no more for him. Or, technically, one more, but we wouldn't be together.

I swallowed and stared into the distance.

The next act was the brass quartet. Sometimes I still wondered if I'd failed Abuelo by not being a part of this group. Hopefully not—I had to believe that the change I'd seen in him was more important than whether I aced one particular audition.

Andrea joined me, saying, "There you are!"

"Hey," I greeted her. "I thought the play went off perfectly."

"Thanks. You should have taken a bow with me. You helped so much, you should get cowriting credit!"

As seriously as she took her art, for her to say that was a huge compliment. I didn't know how to respond, so I turned and watched the stage, a grin on my face.

The quartet began to play, and I heard a music teacher behind me murmur, "What are they playing? I don't recognize it."

"Me either," replied another. "Is this the special surprise that Edwards promised us?"

I grinned. Nobody in the audience was going to recognize tonight's songs, because none of them had ever heard them before. I looked up at Abuelo, watching his face.

His eyes widened. "That is . . . they're playing my music! How?"

I gestured for Abuelo and Andrea to follow me to a secluded area behind a tall hedge, away from any curious passersby but where we could still hear the rise and fall of each note.

"I found a flash drive with the songs you were working on before . . . you know, the end," I said to Abuelo.

Andrea caught on quickly that I was talking to my grandfather, and she smiled as she glanced from me to him.

Even though she couldn't see him, her eyes sparkled as if she could. "So you shared the flash drive with the music department?" she asked.

I nodded and then met Abuelo's gaze. "It was my gift to you," I said softly, my voice beginning to crack. "My way of saying thank you . . . and goodbye."

Abuelo took a long, slow breath. It was probably my imagination, but I could have sworn his eyes glimmered.

"I thought my new songs had died with me."

"Not on my watch," I said.

For a few seconds we just stood there, letting the music wash over us. Abuelo wiped a translucent tear from his cheek. Maybe I did too.

Finally, Andrea hooked me by my elbow and said, "All right, enough of the sob fest. We're missing the concert!"

We headed back out to the main lawn and listened to the rest of the set. When the music ended, the audience broke out into thunderous applause, and Abuelo took a bow right alongside the musicians.

After the cheering died down, Mami called out, "Time for las doce uvas de la suerte!" Cristina, Manny, and a few of their friends got to work passing out tiny mesh bags, each with twelve grapes inside, while Abuela called me over to help Mami and Papi give out cups of sidra to the adults and nonalcoholic apple cider to the kids. That could only mean one thing: it was almost midnight.

"Hey, Benny, what is this?" DeSean asked after I'd finished delivering the last of the apple cider. He passed me a bag of grapes and started untying his own.

"It's tradition," I explained. "Wait until midnight, and then pop 'em in your mouth. If you get all twelve grapes eaten in the first minute, that's lucky. If not, well, you can figure it out."

"Twelve grapes?" he asked in mock horror. "All at once?"

"One for each month of the new year," I replied, absentmindedly opening my own bag. Too bad Abuelo couldn't join us in this. I wondered what would qualify as lucky for him.

"I wonder how many people choke to death at Cuban New Year's parties," Andrea said. "That gives me an idea for a play. Attack of the killer grapes!"

While she talked about murderous fruit come to life, and DeSean cracked up, Abuelo drifted over until he stood by my side. As much fun as I was having, I couldn't help thinking that these would be my last moments with my grandfather.

"I wish this party would never end," I whispered just loud enough for him to hear.

Abuelo nodded, and I could sense that he felt as torn as I did. "Me too."

Somebody let out an exaggerated "Shhhh! It's time!" and everyone checked their watches or phones. There was just over a minute to go. DeSean rushed off to find his family, while mine found their way to me. Andrea's mom joined us and put her arm around Andrea's shoulders.

Manny gave me a high five. "We did it, bro. We pulled off the party of the year."

"Was there ever any doubt?" I replied.

Cristina twirled, smiling smugly as she said, "I don't know about you, but I never doubt myself."

We all laughed at that one, even Cristina.

A few seconds later, the crowd started counting down.

I didn't participate at first, until Manny jostled me and I joined in. I found myself wishing time would stop, but while I'd seen and felt a lot of impossible things over the last four months, time apparently stopped for neither kids nor ghosts.

With each second, I remembered a moment with Abuelo. A time he'd made me angry. A time he'd made me laugh. A time he'd made me believe I had it in me to be a star. I couldn't imagine life without him.

The seconds kept on ticking down, and the closer we got to zero, the more people added their voices.

"THREE . . . TWO . . . ONE . . . HAPPY NEW YEAR!"

I shoved the grapes in my mouth. Even though *wishes* aren't actually a part of the tradition, I found myself making one anyway as I swallowed the last grape.

"Don't choke, mi nieto. Don't become a character in one of your strange friend's stories."

I turned to see Abuelo looking down at me. He was still here. Nothing had happened. What did that mean? I blinked, not daring to even hope for anything, because wanting to keep my abuelo around felt like the ultimate betrayal, after how far he'd come.

A giant spotlight flicked on at that moment, illuminating a patch of concrete right in front of us. I tried to trace the light back to its source but couldn't find one. All around us, people gasped, wondering what further spectacle those creative Ramírezes had decided to save for after midnight.

A door appeared in the middle of the spotlight, popping into existence the same way Abuelo always did: I was looking right at the spot, but I didn't actually see the moment it arrived. One instant there was no door, and the next, it seemed like a door had been there all along.

"Oh wow!"

"How are they doing these special effects!"

"I can't wait to see what Félix does with our end-of-year production!"

"I'm so glad we stayed until midnight!"

"When you guys throw a party, you *really* throw a party!"

"Is that Abuelo?" Cristina asked.

In shock, I glanced at my grandfather, then back to Cristina. "You can see him?" She nodded as she took a step closer.

Meanwhile, Manny tapped my arm over and over again while staring slack-jawed at Abuelo. "Bro, what's going on?"

Suddenly solid, Abuelo took a step into the illuminated circle, his face uncertain for once. He faced the family, their eyes wide and their mouths open.

I moved to stand next to Abuelo. "This is who I've been talking to all those times you thought I was going crazy."

Cristina's head twitched, like a robot with a misfiring circuit. "This . . . this is . . ."

"Is he— Are you . . . a ghost?" Manny asked.

"You could say that," Abuelo said. "But right now, I seem to be a little less . . . ghostly. I'm so glad you can finally see me and hear me, so I can tell you all how wonderful you were tonight, and how proud I am of you." He gave each of them a kiss on the forehead.

"This explains the crazy clothes," Cristina said, her voice weirdly soft.

"And you taking up the trumpet," Manny added, turning to me.

"Well, actually no. *You* were responsible for that. Don't you remember?"

I practically fell over as Andrea skidded into me. "Ohmygod it's him I can really really see him it's Ignacio Ramírez I AM YOUR BIGGEST FAN!"

Abuelo, who had stopped after a single step, turned to look at her. "You like my music? You never mentioned that before."

She blinked. "What? No! I love *ghosts*! I need to talk to you! I have so many questions. Do you leave ectoplasm wherever you go? Where are you when you're not with Benny? Do you sleep? Have you visited anybody you knew before to spy on them while you're invisible? What is it like to—"

I pulled her away. "Please don't scare the ghost, Andrea."

I glanced around the lit spot. Somehow, everybody knew to stay out of the light—everybody except Abuelo, who had lived his life in the spotlight.

At the edge of the circle, Abuela Gloria and Papi had linked arms, and I could see Mami standing behind them, gently pushing them forward.

"Abuelo," I whispered to him, "you know how you were wishing you could tell Papi and Abuela the things you never got to say when you were alive? Well, this might be your only chance."

Abuelo smiled gratefully at me, then moved toward his ex. He tentatively reached out to clasp one of her hands. "Gloria."

She swallowed. "Ignacio."

"You were right about everything," he said. "About the music, and family, and letting things get away from me. If I had the chance to do it all over again, I would skip all the tours and commercial shoots and spend my time with you and Félix. Well, except for that one soda commercial. That one was pretty good, with me in the race car and—"

"Ahem!" I cleared my throat loudly.

"Huh?" He blinked. "Oh, right. Like I was saying, I'm so sorry I let you down, Gloria. Do you forgive me?"

She laughed, a short explosion that seemed to be more shock than amusement. "I do, Ignacio."

Abuelo shifted his gaze to Papi. "Félix, I wasn't the father you deserved, but I couldn't be prouder of the father you turned out to be. You don't have my style . . ." He slicked back his hair with a grin. "Pero tienes un buen corazón. Eso es más importante, ¿verdad?"

With that comment, I was as floored as Papi looked. The man who'd shown up in my room our first night in Miami would never have thought that having a good heart was more important than having good hair. Abuelo really had changed.

An unnaturally loud click drew our attention back to the door, which swung open. Sounds of an even livelier party spilled from the other side. Since there was no wall, just a door, people around the spotlight circle stared, trying to understand how it was possible that there was a room on the other side of it.

A man stepped through, accompanied by a dog.

"Carlos!" Abuelo cried out. "And Iggy 1!"

Manny nudged me. "Wait. Abuelo named *two* dogs after himself?"

Carlos applauded slowly. "Well, Ignacio," he said after a moment, "you surprised me. I didn't think you could, but you proved me wrong. You became a part of your family. You stopped putting stardom before love. You are welcome to join us—we would all love to see the Ignacio Ramírez we remember, from before the fame and the business changed him."

Abuelo swelled up. "Thank you, Carlos. Thank you for giving me this chance. It was a far better gift than you may realize. You gave me my family back."

I felt like I might explode from all the warring feelings I had inside. "Abuelo!" I cried out, the word sounding like a sob.

Suddenly everybody was looking at me. Tears streamed down my face, but I didn't care who saw. I threw my arms around him, finally able to connect, and said, "I won't forget you!"

Abuelo swallowed and turned back toward the door. "Carlos . . . eh . . . you've been very patient with me . . . thank you for coming back . . . eh . . ." He ran a hand along his scalp.

I stared up at him. This was it. The moment we'd worked so hard for. Why was he stalling?

"Spit it out, Ignacio."

"Do I have to go?"

"*What?* Ignacio Ramírez, do you have any idea what a rare opportunity you were given? Do you have any idea how many of us believed you did not deserve this chance at the afterlife? Do you seriously mean to stand there and reject our gift? Are you ready to permanently kiss your chance of moving on goodbye?"

Abuelo took a deep breath. "If that's the way it has to be, Carlos, then yes. Please don't be mad!"

Carlos maintained a stern face for a few more seconds, but it soon dissolved into a smile, and he laughed. "I'm not mad! I'm just messing with you. You can stay if you want."

Abuelo blinked. "Really?"

"Why not?" Carlos shrugged. "You wouldn't be the first spirit to decide to stay behind to watch their kids and grandkids grow up. Ghosts do it all the time. I can check on you again next New Year's!"

Abuelo turned in a slow arc, making eye contact with Gloria, and then Papi and Mami, and finally Cristina, Manny, and me. "I would like that, but only if you all will have me."

I gasped. "What? Of course we will!" I turned to my siblings. "Right?"

They just stared at me skeptically, and I remembered that they'd experienced none of what I had these past months. They hadn't seen all of the growing Abuelo had done behind the scenes; they'd only heard the stories of how he wasn't there for Papi or for Abuela Gloria. But that's when I remembered what Mami had said to me when she asked for my help getting my brother and sister on board for the counseling sessions. *What you think matters to both of them.*

"Trust me," I said. "Our abuelo is pretty cool. If you get to know him, you won't regret it."

Manny and Cristina shared a glance, then nodded in silent agreement. "Okay, we trust you," Cristina said finally. "If he's all right with you, he's all right with us."

"But he can't make me wear any of his clothes!" Manny added.

"Deal," I said with a smile. I turned toward Papi, who'd been hurt the most but who had seen Abuelo's scrapbook too. "What do you say, Papi?"

My father took a ragged breath. "Are you kidding? Spending time with my father again? For so many years it was the only thing I ever wanted! I . . . love you, Papi."

"I love you too, Félix." Abuelo wrapped him in a tight hug that might've lasted a few seconds or an hour.

"Well, there you have it," I told Abuelo when they finally pulled apart. "You're stuck with us. Besides, you haven't finished teaching me to play the trumpet."

EPILOGUE

"Benny, wait!"

I turned in the current of kids desperate to rush home for the weekend and gave Andrea a chance to catch up to me. Since my parents were my ride, there was no real point in hurrying on my part—I'd leave when they left.

Today she had on black jeans with rivets by the pockets and a long-sleeve shirt with an illustration in neon green of an alien, with the caption NEVER MIND, THERE'S NO INTELLIGENT LIFE ON THIS PLANET. I wondered if she had a portal in her closet to allow her to store so many different Goth outfits and funny T-shirts.

Falling into step beside me, she asked, "Did you read your grandfather the latest pages of my new play?"

She'd been working on a show that was basically about me and Abuelo and our experiences since I moved here. Since he couldn't turn the pages, the only way to get his feedback was for me to read the material to him.

"I did," I said. "He liked it a lot, but he's got some notes for you."

"Terrific!"

"You want to come over and hear them?"

Andrea paused right in the middle of the flow, and I had to step over to a bulletin board to keep from being trampled.

She bit her lip. "Yes, but . . ."

"But what?"

"Um, what day this weekend are you doing your homework for my mom's class?"

I laughed. "I was gonna do it tonight. Since the assignment was to cook something with milk, I thought I'd try my grandmother's arroz con leche recipe."

Andrea's mom's comment at the party calling me an artist had gotten me thinking. Over the holiday break, I asked my parents to put in paperwork saying that my artistic needs weren't being fully met. While I still wanted to be in band, I had a second calling: cooking. The school took some convincing, though. The budget cuts that had made them get rid of home economics hadn't changed. Even if they could bring the program back, they didn't usually let students take two art courses at the same time. But after the administrators tasted my spiced beef empanadas, they changed their minds. Since SMPAS was a magnet school, reclassifying home ec as "culinary arts" got it reinstated, and Ms. Wade had even been returned to her former role as the instructor.

Andrea brightened at the mention of dessert. "Well, then, tonight sounds perfect—let me text my mom! I'll even help you prepare the . . . whatever you said—but only so long as you let me taste-test!"

"Okay," I agreed, walking again. "Let me get my trumpet from the band lockers and then we can go meet my parents in the parking lot."

I was getting better the more I played. Maybe somewhere down the line there'd be another special band to audition for, and who knew how I'd do then? But for now I was happy just to make music.

"I came up with a title for the play," Andrea said, keeping pace with me. "*Benny Ramírez and the Nearly Departed.* What do you think?"

I made a face. "I hate it."

"Well, too bad," she said. "It's not up to you, it's my play."

"How is it your play? It's my story! It's my *name*!"

"It may be your story, but I wrote it!"

I rolled my eyes but let it drop. I'd convince her to change it later.

In the car, the four of us were squeezed in like sardines again. It felt even tighter than I remembered. Maybe we were getting bigger. Since Papi was sick of us begging for a minivan, I suggested a stretch limo. He vetoed that too for some reason.

The whole drive, Manny talked about the new card game he wanted to try out tomorrow for Sleepover Saturday, and he didn't stop describing it until we were pulling into the driveway.

We parked next to Abuela's truck, which she had repainted to say CABANA RAMÍREZ: MIAMI'S BEST CUBAN FOOD TO GO. After Abuelo showed up at the party, she had decided to stay, and we were thrilled to have her.

Iggy practically knocked me over when we came through the front door. For some reason, it was always me that he pounced on—he probably still associated me with his improved dog food.

"Welcome home!" Abuela called out. "I'm making caldo gallego. Dinner's in an hour!"

"We can work in the dining room," I said to Andrea. "That way we'll already be there when my grandmother's food is ready."

"I like the way you think!" she said.

"Mi nieto!" Abuelo's voice boomed. "You brought your playwright friend with you!"

"Good!" Abuela said. "Take him with you. For somebody who can't taste, your grandfather certainly has a lot of opinions on what I should put into my caldo!"

Abuelo pretended to look stricken. "I was only trying to be helpful!"

Andrea set her laptop up on the table and opened the file. "So, you say the trumpet-playing ghost was a star, but that's not right," said Abuelo.

Andrea blinked. "It's not?"

"No no no. *Super*star. The biggest. You can spell that, right?"

I scratched behind Iggy's ears and tuned the two of them out. I already knew all about Abuelo's many, many successes.

Most people couldn't remember much about what happened after midnight at the party. Everybody was sure it was the most amazing New Year's party they'd ever attended, but they were all a bit hazy on the details. Specifically, nobody seemed to be talking about the ghost of Ignacio Ramírez putting in an appearance.

The family remembered, though, and now my siblings and parents and Abuela Gloria could all see him.

And then there was Andrea. My best guess was that her obsession with ghosts had made her remember when everybody else could not, and she could see and hear him now, even though sometimes she wished she couldn't.

They focused on Andrea's play, and I focused on the dog, until it was time for the living to wash up and fill their plates.

We always set a place for Abuelo, even though he didn't

need to eat, because he was part of the family, and family belonged at the table. I soaked in the happy noise—the talk about school, or the requests for someone to pass a condiment, or the weekend plans—and thought it was interesting how home can sneak up on you, and you only realize you're there after it's happened.

"How is your play coming along?" Papi asked. "If it's another hit like at the party, SMPAS is going to have a hard time keeping you from leaving us and going to Hollywood."

"And I bet you know just the producer to make her work a hit," Mami added with a wink.

"So far, so good," Andrea said, "but the ending isn't working yet."

"What do you mean?" I asked.

She swallowed a bit of Abuela's stew and said, "I can't decide if the ghost would regret his decision to stay or not."

I leaned toward Abuelo and raised my voice. "Well?"

Abuelo, who had gotten distracted by trying fruitlessly to call Iggy over to him, perked up. "Yes?"

I pointed to Andrea, who straightened.

"Uh, I was wondering. Are you ever sorry you passed up that big party you were supposed to go to?"

I watched Abuelo's face, curious about his answer.

He waved a hand dismissively. "Nah. I got to go to plenty of parties in my time, but the best party is right here."

When Carlos had popped that ghostly door open, I

caught glimpses of well-dressed people and strains of amazing music. What did we have that compared to that?

We had one overcrowded little table that had barely been big enough for five of us back in California, around which sat four kids, two parents, one live grandparent and one ghost, and a dog begging each person for scraps. We had good food and happy noise and people who cared about each other.

Yep, this was a party, all right, and I couldn't imagine a better one.

ACKNOWLEDGMENTS

Thank *you,* reader, for reading this book, and for being curious to know about everybody who helped bring to life this little slice of my hometown.

I want to acknowledge and thank Miami itself, a weird and cool place to grow up. Miami is the city where I spent the first thirty years of my life, and also a place I seem to keep returning to in my fiction. It is a quintessentially American city: a diverse place where individuals and families from all over the world come together to create a lively and exciting community. In this story, I wanted to show a different Miami than movies and television portray. Lots of people know about South Beach and Downtown, about Art Deco and neon. But that's not the part of town where I grew up. I wanted to show my readers mangroves and banyan trees and shady streets. Hopefully, in future books I'll get to show off more of my hometown.

I also want to thank the folks at Working Partners—particularly Chris Snowdon, Elizabeth Galloway, Stephanie Elliott, Crystal Velasquez, James Noble, Clare Hutton, and Dan Jolley—for making this book possible and letting me write it, Kristin Ostby at Greenhouse Literary Agency for enthusiastically putting it in the right hands, and Gianna Lakenauth and the entire Knopf BFYR team for deciding to bring Benny and his family and friends into the world. Thank you all for the hours you spent editing this manuscript and challenging me to go deeper, to give more details, to be funnier. I may possibly have sighed or complained once or twice, but you were right every single time you thought the book needed more. Thanks also to the people doing the behind-the-scenes work, which I don't even know all the details about: Iris Broudy, Artie Bennett, Jake Eldred, Jade Rector, Michelle Crowe, Kim Small, and everyone else who has contributed to the making and promotion of this book in some way. What you do is fascinating and beyond me, and I wish I knew more about it.

I want to thank my agent, Cameron McClure at Donald Maass Literary Agency, for sticking with me for a truly absurd number of years before I finally earned you a dime. *grin* When I was looking for representation, I read books by your other clients and felt like you appreciated the quirky kind of stories I liked to tell, stories that were more about family and friendship and relationships than about heroes and villains. Thank you for believing in me; hopefully, there will be many more books to come after this one.

I've been ridiculously fortunate to have the best group of writing partners anybody could possibly ask for—people who can offer critiques, help me out with the big picture and voice, and also make me believe I can pull this off. You don't get a group like my Owls overnight—it takes many years of growing together, and I'm so glad I've gotten to grow with you. Thank you to Marlana Antifit—founder of the Owls!—who, beyond offering feedback and indefatigable cheerleading, also insisted on making sure I knew what it felt like to hold and play a trumpet and shared with me infinite details about being a musician. Thanks as well to the rest of my Owls and my other beta readers—Mimi Powell, Peggy Jackson, Brian Truitt, Jennye Kamin, Molly McGranahan Hubsch, Stephanie Spier, Vivi Harris Barnes, Ann Meier, Evergreen Lee, and Gary Lee—for your feedback on this manuscript. More than that, thanks for your encouragement, for talking me down off the occasional ledge, and, most important, for your friendship.

Thank you to my kids, Megan and Eleana, grown now, but who had to put up with not one but *two* weirdos constantly going out to writing groups and coffee shops and libraries and science fiction conventions. I remember taking you to playgrounds and letting you run around while I hunkered down with my laptop in a shady spot and tried to ignore the ants. Thank you for never rolling your eyes, and for being as excited as we were for every success.

Most of all, I owe an incalculable amount to my spouse, Lisa Iriarte. And here . . . my words seem inadequate, and I've gone and made myself late turning these acknowledgments in. For more than twenty-six years we've chased our dreams of telling stories and seeing them in print, and we've both gotten to hold our published works in our hands. I can't imagine how much harder it would have been to do all this without a partner who *Got It*. I also can't imagine how I ever would have produced anything publishable without having your own talent and craft to inspire and challenge me. Thank you for being my first and best alpha reader, my voice of reason, and somebody who believed in my writing when I wasn't sure if I did. "Thank you" seems like so much less than needs to be said here. Thank you. I love you.

CREDITS

ALFRED A. KNOPF BOOKS FOR YOUNG READERS

Art and Interior Design
Michelle Crowe

Jade Rector

Contracts
Jacquelyn Marr

Copyeditors and Proofreaders
Artie Bennett

Iris Broudy

Judy Kiviat

Alison Kolani

Lisa Leventer

Editor
Gianna Lakenauth

Managing Editor
Jake Eldred

Marketing
John Adamo
Regina Andreoni
Michelle Campbell
Natalie Capogrossi
Natali Cavanagh
Jasmine Ferrufino
David Gilmore
Katie Halata
Jenn Inzetta
Kelly McGauley
Shannon Pender
Alexandra Schneider
Erica Stone
Stephania Villar
Meredith Wagner
Adrienne Waintraub
Elizabeth Ward

Production Manager
Shameiza Ally

Publicity
Kim Small

Publisher
Melanie Nolan

Sales
A special thank-you to the entire sales division.

GREENHOUSE LITERARY

Kristin Ostby

WORKING PARTNERS

Stephanie Lane Elliott
Crystal Velasquez

TURN THE PAGE FOR A SNEAK PEEK OF AJ TORRES AND THE TREASURE OF CAPTAIN GRAYSHARK!

A SWASHBUCKLING TALE OF FRIENDSHIP, COURAGE, AND GHOST PIRATES!

AJ Torres and the Treasure of Captain Grayshark excerpt text copyright © 2025 by Working Partners Ltd
Cover art copyright © 2025 by Mirelle Ortega
Published by Alfred A. Knopf, an imprint of Random House Children's Books,
a division of Penguin Random House LLC, New York.

PROLOGUE
1725, SOMEWHERE IN THE UPPER KEYS OF FLORIDA

A trio of palm trees receded through the spyglass, shrinking until they disappeared behind the churning sea. On the deck of the *Salty Rogue*, Captain Cornelius Grayshark pulled the scope away from his eye, collapsed it with a satisfied grunt, and turned toward the ship's bow.

"Aye, Ollie, we did it!"

He gave the ship's wheel an exuberant spin, sending the vessel into a turn and earning a squawking rebuke from Ollie, the green-and-orange parrot clinging to the yard.

"The gold, the Compañero Colgante, and the finest ship to ever sail the Caribbean . . . all of it ours, and ours alone!"

The parrot took a couple of fluttering hops and landed on Grayshark's shoulder. "All alone! All alone!"

Grayshark frowned. "Don't be like that, Ollie. We'll 'ire a new crew. An even better crew!" He lashed one of the spokes to the post and marched the width of the deck. "Why, I don't even miss the old crew!"

"Miss the crew!"

"Nay, I don't miss them at all." He leaned a hand on the gunwale and stared out at the open water. "Well, maybe just a little."

The bird hopped to the main deck and squawked.

"Aye," Grayshark agreed softly. "I will miss Yago. He been the closest thing a gentleman o' fortune could possibly 'ave to a friend." He straightened and grinned. "Apart from you, that is! And I still have you, Ollie!"

A gust of wind swept the deck, blowing Grayshark's hat askew. The old pirate peered at the horizon. Was the sky darker now? Aye, it was. It definitely was. On the mast behind him, the sail flapped loudly as rain began to fall.

The *Salty Rogue* lurched, knocking him to his knees. He grabbed the wheel and pulled himself to his feet. He fought to steer as the ship climbed a wave. Grayshark swallowed to keep last night's grog from coming up.

"Keep it together," he admonished himself. "It be just another storm, an' ye be an experienced sailor. Just do what ye always do."

A wave slammed into the port side of the ship, and Ollie took to the air, circled the deck, and landed in front of the hatch.

"Down below! Down below!"

The captain's face heated up. Right. He usually rode out the storm belowdecks, counting on the crew to keep the ship together. But now he *was* the crew. Why hadn't he brought at least *a few* sea dogs along?

The *Salty Rogue* dipped between two waves, and then climbed . . . and climbed. The deck rose so steeply it went nearly vertical, and Grayshark clung desperately to the wheel as his feet slipped out from under him. After the ship slammed down again, he scrambled back to his feet just in time to see a giant wave barreling toward his position.

Something inside Grayshark turned to lead. "That's not good."

"Not good! Not good!" chirped Ollie.

The wave smashed into the *Salty Rogue,* and beams cracked and snapped around him. The deck leaned perilously starboard and groaned as the ship struggled to right itself. Just when it seemed she might pull through, the port cannons tore loose from their mountings and slid across the deck, shifting their weight and suspending the ship at a lopsided angle. A second wave hit right then, and the *Salty Rogue* capsized, launching Grayshark into the sea.

He flailed in the churning water. He knew it was a bit of a liability for a pirate, but he'd never been a good swimmer. Still, he could probably reach one of the surrounding islands if he tried.

But his treasure was still aboard the ship! And here he was, the greatest pirate in the Caribbean, about to drown at sea before spending a single coin of it. How embarrassing! "This isn't how it ends for me!" he sputtered.

As if to say, *Yes, it is,* a high crest slapped his chest. Coughing out seawater, he scanned the waves until, finally, he spotted it: the broken section of the *Rogue* where he'd stashed his treasure! It bobbed and drifted, just out of reach. His spirits soared. If he could get to it, he might not merely survive, but survive with his booty intact!

He fought his way across the waves and felt deep relief when at last he laid a hand on the torn wooden planking.

"Saved!" he grunted, not sure if he meant the chest filled with gold coins and the Spanish pendant, or his life. It didn't matter . . . he'd escape with both.

That's when he felt something tug at his leg. He turned back just as a bolt of lightning flashed, and his heart seized in dread. Captain Grayshark found himself staring into the face of a giant squid, its angry, intelligent eyes focused on the tentacle wrapped around his ankle. Grayshark grabbed the hull and pulled, trying to free himself, but the creature seemed to be elastic. It pulled back with such force that Grayshark's fingers slipped off the hull of his broken ship. He opened his mouth to scream but succeeded only in swallowing a mouthful of saltwater. A faint gurgle sounded as he was dragged beneath the surface and into the murky depths of the sea.

GRAYSHARK AWOKE... THOUGH he didn't remember falling asleep. All he knew was that he was fully alert now. Even stranger, he was on his feet... and dry.

He turned and examined his surroundings. Thick foliage limited his view to just a few feet in each direction. Cypress, oak, and mangrove. Not a living soul or a pint of ale in sight. Still, compared to being in the middle of a raging sea with an angry squid, this was paradise! He gave a joyful little hop. It felt like he could fly if he just thought about it hard enough.

Speaking of flying... he pinched his lips together and whistled out two short blasts followed by a high trill. For one tense moment nothing happened, and then a rush of wings fluttered beside him as Ollie landed on his shoulder.

"You made it, too, old friend!" He turned a little jig, making the bird flap to keep his perch.

"We survived! Old Davy Jones may have his day with us eventually, but not today! We still be here!"

Grayshark took a few more steps, trying to get his bearings. He headed in the direction of the surf, marveling at how little soreness he felt after his ordeal. As he brushed aside a palm frond, a familiar formation caught his eye: a gnarled knot in a banyan tree that looked more like a wooden mermaid, pointing east.

Grayshark's breath caught. He *knew* this tree. He'd used it before, as a landmark!

"Ollie! We be saved! This here be me island!" He picked up his pace, crashing through the foliage with abandon, now that he knew where he was. He'd landed on the same island where he'd last seen his crew, asleep and three sheets to the wind! He couldn't remember how he'd come to be separated from them, but who cared? He was back, and he knew they'd welcome their captain with open arms. They would get off this island—together, this time.

Pushing into a clearing, he spotted three men walking toward him. When he saw Yago out in front, his beard scraggly as ever, Grayshark shouted happily, "There 'e be! Yago!"

But the glare on Yago's face made him pause. He'd never seen his first mate look so . . . angry, and he was heading straight for him.

"Oh, I get it!" Grayshark said. "Ye be upset because ye been worried about me. Bucko, me hearty, ye can stop worrying! I'm alive! *We're* alive!" He spread his arms wide to greet his old friend with a hug.

That's when Yago *walked right through him,* leaving an icy sensation behind as he climbed to higher ground.

Grayshark froze. Had Yago . . . had he just walked *through* him? That wasn't good.

"It's as though I be not 'ere," he said softly.

"Not here! Not here!" Ollie called out mournfully.

The captain held his head, suddenly not feeling so well.

Two sickening thoughts sped through his mind, like racing frigatebirds. First, *Am I* dead? And more important, *WHERE IS MY TREASURE?*

CHAPTER ONE

The pirate glared at me with one glassy blue eye. The other was covered with a black leather patch that matched his boots.

"There isn't room enough for the two of us on this here poop deck, ye scallywag!" I growled, raising my sword over my head. "Walk the plank!"

Jayden let out a big sigh. "AJ, can you stop goofing around, bro? The tournament's about to start."

I lowered my sword, which was really a bright yellow golf club, and said, "Fine. Whatever you say, Cap'n." I gave the pirate statue that stood guard at the entrance to Rubén's Pirate Adventure Mini Golf Course a halfhearted salute and followed my best friend inside.

"Good. Now get your head in the game," Jayden demanded. "There's a lot at stake."

He didn't need to remind me. Just the other morning, he had woken me up with the worst news ever: His mom had been laid off, and she was looking for a new job out of town.

"You mean like Fort Lauderdale? Boca?" I'd asked.

He'd shaken his head sadly and muttered, "More like Jacksonville, where my grandparents live."

After doing a few quick calculations in my mind, I became so upset that I jumped out of bed, not even embarrassed that I was still rocking my superhero pajama shorts. "But that's, like, three hundred fifty miles away! At least five hours by car. It might as well be another planet!"

"I know." Jayden had nodded as he sat heavily in my desk chair and extended his long legs in front of him.

"And that means . . ."

"I might move," he'd finished.

I couldn't even picture Jayden not living next door to me. He always had, and since his mom worked long hours, he spent almost as much time in my house as in his own. All of a sudden, that would be over.

"What about school?" I'd asked.

"I guess I'll have to transfer somewhere else before the summer's out."

Somehow that was even more of a gut punch. We were already a few weeks into our summer vacation, so summer would be over in no time. Plus, not to brag, but Jayden Williams and yours truly, Alejandro Javier Torres, were big deals at SMPAS—South Miami Performing Arts School. Since his breakthrough performance as a possessed fish stick in Andrea Wade's play about a haunted lunchroom, he'd become the most sought-after actor in the seventh grade, next to Manny Ramírez. And the way I'd managed to rig the frozen foods using some polyurethane cord and a pulley system so that they'd looked like they were floating had gotten me promoted to Junior Assistant Associate Set Designer Number Three for all the school plays. Only twelve years old, and we practically ran the place. He couldn't leave now!

"Is there anything we can do to get your mom to stay here?" I'd asked.

Jayden had scoffed. "Sure. Come up with enough cash to pay our rent and bills for a few months and find my mom a job in town."

I couldn't do much about the job, unless she wanted to stand on the side of the road and twirl a giant cardboard sign that read IT'S NOT TOURISM . . . IT'S TORRESM! I'd happily relinquish that position—and the alligator costume it came with—to her, but my parents seemed to think it was important for me to participate in the family travel business. I did have an idea for how we could come up with the cash, though—at least some of it.

That's how we'd ended up at Rubén's Pirate Adventure

Mini Golf Course near Miami Beach a couple days later, competing to win a $300 cash prize. Luckily, even though Hurricane Belinda was due to skirt the coast any day now, and some businesses had already closed in preparation, the tournament went on as planned.

That's because the course was run by none other than Rubén Vega. He'd become a local celebrity for regularly roaming his property in full-on pirate cosplay. As a theater kid, I couldn't help but be impressed by his commitment to the bit. He greeted his customers rocking a giant hat, a wig of long black hair, a sword, a big red coat, and even a fake peg leg that covered one of his real legs. He was barely taller than me, though, and his belly bulging against his ruffled shirt made him look more like somebody's uncle than a swashbuckling pirate. But he refused to let a hurricane scare him off, so I guess that was something.

He had a giant button, at least six inches across, on his coat that read ARRRRRRRSSSSK ME ABOUT CAPTAIN GRAYSHARRRRK in bold black letters against a white background. Jayden and I knew better than to do anything of the sort. Rubén was *really* into pirate history, and if you gave him half a chance, he would talk at you about it for hours. Worse, he'd try to get you to visit the adjoining museum that he'd curated himself, dedicated to local maritime history and the pirates who once sailed the waters around Florida. It was a giant snoozefest I only barely remembered from our second-grade school trip. The only reason anyone put up with Rubén's conversational whirlpools was because the golf course was low-key amazing.

"Welcome to our Semi-Annual Pirate Adventure Golf Tournament!" he called out now over the bullhorn. "Teams who preregistered, go get your clubs. Everybody else, head for Snappy. Yarr."

That was literally how he said it—"Yarr," not *"YARR!"*

He pointed to a podium in the shape of a giant Day-Glo green alligator standing on its hind legs. Rubén's assistant, a bored-looking teenage girl who was chewing gum and writing furiously on a notepad, stood on the platform, which made it look like she was getting a piggyback ride from the gator.

As she explained the app Rubén had set up where scores would be updated throughout the course of the game, I glanced around, sizing up the competition: a few tourists who didn't look like they'd ever held golf clubs before, an elderly couple with thick bifocals, a group of college kids who seemed way more interested in taking selfies with the fake pirates . . . I liked our chances.

That is, until I noticed who was standing in line right in front of us, waiting to sign up with her friend.

"Is that . . . ?" I whispered to Jayden.

"Cristina Ramírez," Jayden whispered back with a nod. Already his face was flushed, and his breathing sped up, like he was on the verge of hyperventilating. Oh no. Of all the school kids for us to run into, it had to be Cristina, the object of Jayden's massive crush. He was usually cool and laid-back, the definition of unbothered, but in Cristina's presence, he turned into a nervous ball of sweat.

"Get it together, bro," I said under my breath.

Jayden nodded and furiously wiped his hands on his shirt, just as Cristina finished signing up and noticed the two of us.

"Oh, hey, guys!" she said with a friendly wave. "Are you entering too?"

Jayden's mouth opened and closed a couple times, like a robot whose operating system had crashed, but no sound came out.

"Yes," I jumped in. "And we're going to demolish you."

Cristina shared an amused look with her friend, a tall redhead with freckles named Sarah, who I also recognized as a ballet dancer from SMPAS.

"Oh yeah?" said Cristina. "Well, bring it on."

After they floated away and I finished signing us up and downloading the app, Jayden groaned miserably. "How could you jinx us by telling her we were going to demolish them?"

"It's called trash talk, Jayden. And it works! We've got them shaking in their ballet slippers."

We didn't. Cristina and Sarah were giggling as they took a few practice putts, looking super relaxed, but Jayden, who looked like he had just taken a dip in the Atlantic, didn't need to hear that.

We chose our golf balls and followed a path of paving stones to the first hole, where pirate figures held bottles of grog or swords in one hand and bags of coins or bejeweled necklaces in the other. They were having a blast. The people of the town they'd just sacked were probably not as thrilled, but for some reason, we never really talked about them.

I leaned forward to watch the first team get started.

One of the college kids, in a Miami Dolphins jersey and ball cap, sank the very first ball in two shots, and his teammate high-fived him. The elderly couple made par too. I guess it made sense that nobody would sign up for a tournament unless they were pretty good. Cristina and her friend were no different, except before they took their turn, Sarah loudly said, "Show 'em how it's done." Cristina did just that by getting a hole in one, and Sarah squealed.

Okay, so this was not going to be as easy as I'd hoped.